DELINQUENCY AND CRIMINAL BEHAVIOR

GENERAL EDITORS

Dale C. Garell, M.D.
Medical Director, California Children Services, Department of Health Services,
    County of Los Angeles
Associate Dean for Curriculum; Clinical Professor, Department of Pediatrics &
    Family Medicine, University of Southern California School of Medicine
Former President, Society for Adolescent Medicine

Solomon H. Snyder, M.D.
Distinguished Service Professor of Neuroscience, Pharmacology, and Psychiatry,
    Johns Hopkins University School of Medicine
Former President, Society for Neuroscience
Albert Lasker Award in Medical Research, 1978

CONSULTING EDITORS

Robert W. Blum, M.D., Ph.D.
Professor and Director, Division of General Pediatrics and Adolescent Health,
    University of Minnesota

Charles E. Irwin, Jr., M.D.
Professor of Pediatrics; Director, Division of Adolescent Medicine, University of
    California, San Francisco

Lloyd J. Kolbe, Ph.D.
Director of the Division of Adolescent and School Health, Center for Chronic
    Disease Prevention and Health Promotion, Centers for Disease Control

Jordan J. Popkin
Director, Division of Federal Employee Occupational Health, U.S. Public Health
    Service Region I

Joseph L. Rauh, M.D.
Professor of Pediatrics and Medicine, Adolescent Medicine, Children's Hospital
    Medical Center, Cincinnati
Former President, Society for Adolescent Medicine

THE ENCYCLOPEDIA OF HEALTH

PSYCHOLOGICAL DISORDERS AND THEIR TREATMENT

Solomon H. Snyder, M.D. · General Editor

DELINQUENCY AND CRIMINAL BEHAVIOR

Ellen Heath Grinney

Introduction by C. Everett Koop, M.D., Sc.D.

former Surgeon General, U. S. Public Health Service

CHELSEA HOUSE PUBLISHERS

New York · Philadelphia

The goal of the ENCYCLOPEDIA OF HEALTH *is to provide general information in the ever-changing areas of physiology, psychology, and related medical issues. The titles in this series are not intended to take the place of the professional advice of a physician or other health care professional.*

CHELSEA HOUSE PUBLISHERS
EDITOR-IN-CHIEF   Remmel Nunn
MANAGING EDITOR   Karyn Gullen Browne
COPY CHIEF   Mark Rifkin
PICTURE EDITOR   Adrian G. Allen
ART DIRECTOR   Maria Epes
ASSISTANT ART DIRECTOR   Howard Brotman
MANUFACTURING DIRECTOR   Gerald Levine
SYSTEMS MANAGER   Lindsey Ottman
PRODUCTION MANAGER   Joseph Romano
PRODUCTION COORDINATOR   Marie Claire Cebrián

The Encyclopedia of Health
SENIOR EDITOR   Brian Feinberg

Staff for DELINQUENCY AND CRIMINAL BEHAVIOR
ASSOCIATE EDITOR   LaVonne Carlson-Finnerty
SENIOR COPY EDITOR   Laurie Kahn
EDITORIAL ASSISTANT   Tamar Levovitz
PICTURE RESEARCHER   Sandy Jones
DESIGNER   Robert Yaffe

3   5   7   9   8   6   4   2

Library of Congress Cataloging-in-Publication Data

Grinney, Ellen Heath
    Delinquency and criminal behavior/by Ellen Heath Grinney; introduction by C. Everett Koop.
        p. cm.—(The Encyclopedia of health. Psychological disorders and their treatment)
    Includes bibliographical references and index.
    Summary: Discusses the origins of delinquent behavior and the social and legal systems developed to deal with it.
    ISBN 0-7910-0045-1
        0-7910-0511-9 (pbk.)
    1. Juvenile delinquency—United States—Juvenile literature. [1. Juvenile delinquency.] I. Title. II. Series.   91-32544
HV9104.G73 1992   CIP
364.3'6'0973—dc20   AC

CONTENTS

THE ENCYCLOPEDIA OF
H E A L T H

THE HEALTHY BODY

The Circulatory System
Dental Health
The Digestive System
The Endocrine System
Exercise
Genetics & Heredity
The Human Body: An Overview
Hygiene
The Immune System
Memory & Learning
The Musculoskeletal System
The Nervous System
Nutrition
The Reproductive System
The Respiratory System
The Senses
Sleep
Speech & Hearing
Sports Medicine
Vision
Vitamins & Minerals

THE LIFE CYCLE

Adolescence
Adulthood
Aging
Childhood
Death & Dying
The Family
Friendship & Love
Pregnancy & Birth

MEDICAL ISSUES

Careers in Health Care
Environmental Health
Folk Medicine
Health Care Delivery
Holistic Medicine
Medical Ethics
Medical Fakes & Frauds
Medical Technology
Medicine & the Law
Occupational Health
Public Health

PSYCHOLOGICAL DISORDERS AND THEIR TREATMENT

Anxiety & Phobias
Child Abuse
Compulsive Behavior
Delinquency & Criminal Behavior
Depression
Diagnosing & Treating Mental Illness
Eating Habits & Disorders
Learning Disabilities
Mental Retardation
Personality Disorders
Schizophrenia
Stress Management
Suicide

MEDICAL DISORDERS AND THEIR TREATMENT

AIDS
Allergies
Alzheimer's Disease
Arthritis
Birth Defects
Cancer
The Common Cold
Diabetes
Emergency Medicine
Gynecological Disorders
Headaches
The Hospital
Kidney Disorders
Medical Diagnosis
The Mind-Body Connection
Mononucleosis and Other Infectious Diseases
Nuclear Medicine
Organ Transplants
Pain
Physical Handicaps
Poisons & Toxins
Prescription & OTC Drugs
Sexually Transmitted Diseases
Skin Disorders
Stroke & Heart Disease
Substance Abuse
Tropical Medicine

PREVENTION AND EDUCATION: THE KEYS TO GOOD HEALTH

C. Everett Koop, M.D., Sc.D.
former Surgeon General,
U.S. Public Health Service

The issue of health education has received particular attention in recent years because of the presence of AIDS in the news. But our response to this particular tragedy points up a number of broader issues that doctors, public health officials, educators, and the public face. In particular, it points up the necessity for sound health education for citizens of all ages.

Over the past 25 years this country has been able to bring about dramatic declines in the death rates for heart disease, stroke, accidents, and for people under the age of 45, cancer. Today, Americans generally eat better and take better care of themselves than ever before. Thus, with the help of modern science and technology, they have a better chance of surviving serious—even catastrophic—illnesses. That's the good news.

But, like every phonograph record, there's a flip side, and one with special significance for young adults. According to a report issued in 1979 by Dr. Julius Richmond, my predecessor as Surgeon General, Americans aged 15 to 24 had a higher death rate in 1979 than they did 20 years earlier. The causes: violent death and injury, alcohol and drug abuse, unwanted pregnancies, and sexually transmitted diseases. Adolescents are particularly vulnerable because they are beginning to explore their own sexuality and perhaps to experiment with drugs. The need for educating young people is critical, and the price of neglect is high.

Yet even for the population as a whole, our health is still far from what it could be. Why? A 1974 Canadian government report attributed all death and disease to four broad elements: inadequacies in the health care system, behavioral factors or unhealthy life-styles, environmental hazards, and human biological factors.

To be sure, there are diseases that are still beyond the control of even our advanced medical knowledge and techniques. And despite yearnings that are as old as the human race itself, there is no "fountain of youth" to ward off aging and death. Still, there is a solution to many of the problems that undermine sound health. In a word, that solution is prevention. Prevention, which includes health promotion and education, saves lives, improves the quality of life, and in the long run, saves money.

In the United States, organized public health activities and preventive medicine have a long history. Important milestones in this country or foreign breakthroughs adopted in the United States include the improvement of sanitary procedures and the development of pasteurized milk in the late 19th century and the introduction in the mid-20th century of effective vaccines against polio, measles, German measles, mumps, and other once-rampant diseases. Internationally, organized public health efforts began on a wide-scale basis with the International Sanitary Conference of 1851, to which 12 nations sent representatives. The World Health Organization, founded in 1948, continues these efforts under the aegis of the United Nations, with particular emphasis on combating communicable diseases and the training of health care workers.

Despite these accomplishments, much remains to be done in the field of prevention. For too long, we have had a medical care system that is science- and technology-based, focused, essentially, on illness and mortality. It is now patently obvious that both the social and the economic costs of such a system are becoming insupportable.

Implementing prevention—and its corollaries, health education and promotion—is the job of several groups of people.

First, the medical and scientific professions need to continue basic scientific research, and here we are making considerable progress. But increased concern with prevention will also have a decided impact on how primary care doctors practice medicine. With a shift to health-based rather than morbidity-based medicine, the role of the "new physician" will include a healthy dose of patient education.

Second, practitioners of the social and behavioral sciences— psychologists, economists, city planners—along with lawyers, business leaders, and government officials—must solve the practical and ethical dilemmas confronting us: poverty, crime, civil rights, literacy, education, employment, housing, sanitation, environmental protection, health care delivery systems, and so forth. All of these issues affect public health.

Third is the public at large. We'll consider that very important group in a moment.

Fourth, and the linchpin in this effort, is the public health profession—doctors, epidemiologists, teachers—who must harness the professional expertise of the first two groups and the common sense and cooperation of the third, the public. They must define the problems statistically and qualitatively and then help us set priorities for finding the solutions.

To a very large extent, improving those statistics is the responsibility of every individual. So let's consider more specifically what the role of the individual should be and why health education is so important to that role. First, and most obvious, individuals can protect themselves from illness and injury and thus minimize their need for professional medical care. They can eat nutritious food; get adequate exercise; avoid tobacco, alcohol, and drugs; and take prudent steps to avoid accidents. The proverbial "apple a day keeps the doctor away" is not so far from the truth, after all.

Second, individuals should actively participate in their own medical care. They should schedule regular medical and dental checkups. Should they develop an illness or injury, they should know when to treat themselves and when to seek professional help. To gain the maximum benefit from any medical treatment that they do require, individuals must become partners in that treatment. For instance, they should understand the effects and side effects of medications. I counsel young physicians that there is no such thing as too much information when talking with patients. But the corollary is the patient must know enough about the nuts and bolts of the healing process to understand what the doctor is telling him or her. That is at least partially the patient's responsibility.

Education is equally necessary for us to understand the ethical and public policy issues in health care today. Sometimes individuals will encounter these issues in making decisions about their own treatment or that of family members. Other citizens may encounter them as jurors in medical malpractice cases. But we all become involved, indirectly, when we elect our public officials, from school board members to the president. Should surrogate parenting be legal? To what extent is drug testing desirable, legal, or necessary? Should there be public funding for family planning, hospitals, various types of medical research, and other medical care for the indigent? How should we allocate scant technological resources, such as kidney dialysis and organ transplants? What is the proper role of government in protecting the rights of patients?

What are the broad goals of public health in the United States today? In 1980, the Public Health Service issued a report aptly entitled *Promoting Health—Preventing Disease: Objectives for the Nation*. This report expressed its goals in terms of mortality and in terms of intermediate goals in education and health improvement. It identified 15 major concerns: controlling high blood pressure; improving family planning; improving pregnancy care and infant health; increasing the rate of immunization; controlling sexually transmitted diseases; controlling the presence of toxic agents and radiation in the environment; improving occupational safety and health; preventing accidents; promoting water fluoridation and dental health; controlling infectious diseases; decreasing smoking; decreasing alcohol and drug abuse; improving nutrition; promoting physical fitness and exercise; and controlling stress and violent behavior.

For healthy adolescents and young adults (ages 15 to 24), the specific goal was a 20% reduction in deaths, with a special focus on motor vehicle injuries and alcohol and drug abuse. For adults (ages 25 to 64), the aim was 25% fewer deaths, with a concentration on heart attacks, strokes, and cancers.

Smoking is perhaps the best example of how individual behavior can have a direct impact on health. Today, cigarette smoking is recognized as the single most important preventable cause of death in our society. It is responsible for more cancers and more cancer deaths than any other known agent; is a prime risk factor for heart and blood vessel disease, chronic bronchitis, and emphysema; and is a frequent cause of complications in pregnancies and of babies born prematurely, underweight, or with potentially fatal respiratory and cardiovascular problems.

Since the release of the Surgeon General's first report on smoking in 1964, the proportion of adult smokers has declined substantially, from 43% in 1965 to 30.5% in 1985. Since 1965, 37 million people have quit smoking. Although there is still much work to be done if we are to become a "smoke-free society," it is heartening to note that public health and public education efforts—such as warnings on cigarette packages and bans on broadcast advertising—have already had significant effects.

In 1835, Alexis de Tocqueville, a French visitor to America, wrote, "In America the passion for physical well-being is general." Today, as then, health and fitness are front-page items. But with the greater scientific and technological resources now available to us, we are in a far stronger position to make good health care available to everyone. And with the greater technological threats to us as we approach the 21st century, the need to do so is more urgent than ever before. Comprehensive information about basic biology, preventive medicine, medical and surgical treatments, and related ethical and public policy issues can help you arm yourself with the knowledge you need to be healthy throughout your life.

FOREWORD

Solomon H. Snyder, M.D.

Mental disorders represent the number one health problem for the United States and probably for the entire human population. Some studies estimate that approximately one-third of all Americans suffer from some sort of emotional disturbance. Depression of varying severity will affect as many as 20% of all of us at one time or another in our lives. Severe anxiety is even more common.

Adolescence is a time of particular susceptibility to emotional problems. Teenagers are undergoing significant changes in their brain as well as their physical structure. The hormones that alter the organs of reproduction during puberty also influence the way we think and feel. At a purely psychological level, adolescents must cope with major upheavals in their lives. After years of not noticing the opposite sex, they find themselves romantically attracted but must painfully learn the skills of social interchange both for superficial, flirtatious relationships and for genuine intimacy. Teenagers must develop new ways of relating to their parents. Adolescents strive for independence. Yet, our society is structured in such a way that teenagers must remain dependent on their parents for many more years. During adolescence, young men and women examine their own intellectual bents and begin to plan the type of higher education and vocation they believe they will find most fulfilling.

Because of these challenges, teenagers are more emotionally volatile than adults. Passages from extreme exuberance to dejection are common. The emotional distress of completely normal adolescence can be so severe that the same disability in an adult would be labeled as major mental illness. Although most teenagers somehow muddle through and emerge unscathed, a number of problems are more frequent among adolescents than among adults. Many psychological aberrations reflect severe disturbances, although these are sometimes not regarded as "psychiatric." Eating disorders, to which young adults are especially vulnerable, are an example. An extremely large number of teenagers diet to great excess even though they are not overweight. Many of them suffer from a specific disturbance referred to as anorexia nervosa, a form of self-starvation that is just as real a disorder as diabetes. The same is true for those who eat compulsively and then sometimes force themselves to vomit. They may be afflicted with bulimia.

Depression is also surprisingly frequent among adolescents, although its symptoms may be less obvious in young people than they are in adults. And, because suicide occurs most frequently in those suffering from depression, we must be on the lookout for subtle hints of despondency in those close to us. This is especially urgent because teenage suicide is a rapidly worsening national problem.

The volumes on Psychological Disorders and Their Treatment in the ENCYCLOPEDIA OF HEALTH cover the major areas of mental illness, from mild to severe. They also emphasize the means available for getting help. *Anxiety and Phobias, Depression,* and *Schizophrenia* deal specifically with these forms of mental disturbance. *Child Abuse* and *Delinquency and Criminal Behavior* explore abnormalities of behavior that may stem from environmental and social influences as much as from biological or psychological illness. *Personality Disorders* and *Compulsive Behavior* explain how people develop disturbances of their overall personality. *Learning Disabilities* investigates disturbances of the mind that may reflect neurological derangements as much as psychological abnormalities. *Mental Retardation* explains the various causes of this many-sided handicap, including the genetic component, complications during pregnancy, and traumas during birth. *Suicide* discusses the epidemiology of this tragic phenomenon and outlines the assistance available to those who are at risk. *Stress Management* locates the source of stress in contemporary society and considers formal strategies for coping with it. Finally, *Diagnosing and Treating Mental Illness* explains to the reader how professionals sift through various signs and symptoms to define the exact nature of the various mental disorders and fully describes the most effective means of alleviating them.

Fortunately, when it comes to psychological disorders, knowing the facts is a giant step toward solving the problems.

CHAPTER 1

A NEW NAME FOR AN OLD PROBLEM

For centuries people did not treat children with special care and attention. The needs of young people have been acknowledged only gradually.

To be young is to be mischievous. There has probably never been a time in history when young people did not occasionally steal, damage private property, run away from home or school, assault other people, or act disrespectful to adults. In fact, the worst of youthful behavior has changed very little throughout civilization; what has changed is society's attitude toward it.

According to *Webster's Ninth New Collegiate Dictionary*, the term *juvenile delinquency* originated in the year 1816. It is defined as juvenile conduct "characterized by antisocial behavior that is beyond parental control and therefore subject to legal action." This definition reveals that 19th-century American society had decided it was appropriate to take legal action against unacceptable youthful behavior. What the definition does not reveal is that ideas about what that legal action should be were changing rapidly.

In the modern mind, childhood is a very specific and relatively carefree period of time that extends from infancy to adolescence. Because children are not as big, as educated, or as experienced as adults

Throughout history children have often been depicted as miniature versions of adults. Renaissance painter Peter Paul Rubens (1577–1640) portrayed his sons wearing adult fashions.

are, less is expected of them. Educators, psychiatrists, psychologists, and physicians have written numerous books and articles for parents offering advice about how to nourish children properly; how to educate and discipline them; how to impart family values; and how to prepare them to make a living, raise their own families, and become good citizens.

But attitudes toward children have not always shown such concern. Throughout early history, people made no major distinction between childhood and adulthood, did not find children particularly appealing or amusing, and did not acknowledge any special responsibilities for their physical or moral welfare. In Western civilization, this disinterest in children was the norm until the Middle Ages drew to a close. In the 400 years that followed, Western civilization developed a whole new concept of who children are, how they should be raised, and, eventually, how they should be punished for wrongdoing.

BEFORE CHILDHOOD EXISTED

The art of every era provides visible evidence of the prevailing attitude toward children. Philippe Ariès, in his book *Centuries of Childhood*, points out that the paintings of the Middle Ages (specifically the period from A.D. 500 to about 1400) rarely present a child that actually looks like a child. Dressed in adult clothes, children in medieval paintings usually look like mature midgets. Ariès cites one painting that shows Isaac, a character in the Old Testament, sitting between his 2 wives, "surrounded by some 15 little men who came up to the level of the grown-ups' waists"—Isaac's children. Most of the paintings of the Madonna and child show a woman stiffly holding a tiny, alert, and dignified creature with adultlike proportions in miniature.

As Western civilization began to awaken intellectually from the stagnation of the Middle Ages, its ideas about children began to change. According to LaMar T. Empey, a national expert on juvenile delinquency, the art of the 16th and 17th centuries clearly shows that people were beginning to view children differently—as though they were looking at "young humans through a different pair of spectacles." Portraits commissioned by the wealthy showed youngsters in special

Society for the Protection of Destitute Roman Catholic Children,

(FOR GIRLS,)

Located at Westchester. Office, No. 25 Chambers street.

Religious thinkers made many early efforts to improve conditions for children, a practice that continues to the present. The British Society for the Protection of Destitute Roman Catholic Children sponsored this ad in 1869.

costumes rather than the clothing of adults, and their bodies looked more like those of children. The literature of the time introduced a tendency to attribute children with endearing qualities that had not been recognized before.

CIVILIZATION'S NEW HOPE

As Europe approached the Renaissance, a powerful group of leaders also began to focus attention on children in an entirely new way. These men were a small minority of moralists, teachers, and churchmen, both Catholic and Protestant, who were disturbed by the corruption of society. In the past, religious thinkers typically retreated from the world's evils to a nunnery or a monastery. By the beginning of the Renaissance, however, they wanted to carry higher standards of morality into subsequent generations.

During the Renaissance, the Christian ideal of the innocence and frailty of children became popular. The color white became a symbol of innocence: When children died, they were buried in white coffins, and they and their funeral attendants were dressed in white. Children became a symbol of godly qualities and good luck. As chubby little cherubs began to appear in Renaissance art, more emphasis was placed on treating children lovingly, controlling them sternly, and guarding their moral welfare. Ariès points out that by the 17th century, women cuddled children more often, and people generally began to consider children cute and amusing.

Yet life during this time remained extremely difficult for young people. A large number of babies were stillborn, and many others died during infancy and childhood. Seventeenth-century women typically did not form the strong, nurturing attachments to their children that are now part of the idealized view of motherhood: They could not afford to become too emotionally attached to each child because so few survived. The wealthy hired wet nurses to nurse and care for their infants. In the homes of the poor, children were often neglected in the chaos of communal living. Nevertheless, the idea gradually developed that a child needs physical, moral, and intellectual caretaking to be properly prepared for adulthood.

EARLY DELINQUENT BEHAVIOR

Despite the growing interest in and concern about them, children continued to suffer abuse and neglect—and to wreak havoc on society. Empey proposes that young people of the Middle Ages and Renaissance learned and used obscenities as early as they could talk. The older ones drank freely in taverns and engaged in sex. Children wore and used arms—even five-year-old boys were known to carry swords as weapons.

Few children ever went to school, and those who did were easily distracted from their studies. In 17th-century France, Empey reports, there were so many mutinies, duels, brawls, and beatings of teachers that students were eventually forbidden to have firearms, swords, or clubs in their rooms or to bring them to class. In England, student rebellions were occasionally put down by troops armed with bayonets.

This 19th-century wood-cut of a London slum scene depicts children behaving in a way that people considered rowdy and uncontrolled.

Although most French students had quit drinking on a regular basis by the 18th century, many English students continued to frequent the pubs well into the 19th century.

PUNISHMENT IN THE OLD WORLD

In 18th-century England, children who committed crimes were routinely hanged, disfigured, whipped, and thrown into prison, just as adults were. In some cases, they were removed to *hulks*, the abandoned and rotting ships anchored offshore for use as floating prisons. In his book *Juvenile Offenders for a Thousand Years*, Wiley B. Sanders describes the wretchedness of children being transported to these ships:

> After having pined and rotted in their respective county [jails] . . . from three months to as many years . . . some [prisoners] are chained on tops of coaches; others, as from London, travel in open caravan, ex-

posed to the inclemency of the weather, to the gaze of
the idle and the taunts and mockeries of the cruel. . . .
Men and boys, children just emerging from infancy,
as young in vice as in years, are fettered together, and
. . . paraded through the kingdom. . . . [They are] ragged
and sickly and carrying in their countenance proofs of
the miseries they had undergone.

Some of these children were also torn from whatever families they
may have had and transported to prison colonies in Australia. Sanders
notes that between 1812 and 1817, 780 males and 136 females, all
under the age of 21, were removed from England in this fashion. Five
of these were age 11, 7 were age 12, 17 were age 13, 32 were age 14,
and 65 were age 15.

FREE FROM EVIL—THE NEW WORLD

Meanwhile, a different sort of traveler had crossed the Atlantic Ocean
to create a new and better world. Leaving England in the early 1600s,
the Puritans hoped to escape the evils of Europe by starting their own
society in America.

One of the evils attributed to the Old World was the corruption and
ungoverned behavior of young people. For example, John Winthrop,
the first governor of the Massachusetts Bay colony, lamented that
"most children, even the best wits and fairest hopes, are perverted,
corrupted, and utterly overthrown." He even went so far as to explain
the Puritan migration to America as a way, at least in part, to help the
young escape the corruption of the Old World.

The Puritans had great faith that each family would be able to raise
its children to be industrious and morally upright adults who would
work to improve the New World. Every unmarried person, child or
adult, was required to live within a family. In 1642, the Massachusetts
Bay colony passed a law requiring parents to teach their children to
read and to maintain a trade. If parents failed at this task, they would
be brought before the authorities. According to Empey, the colonists
had decided that the family should serve as the "guardian of the public
as well as the private good."

In the New World, the Puritans established laws requiring youngsters to learn a trade. Putting children to work continued into the 20th century, as seen in this 1905 photograph of boys stoking a glass-factory furnace.

Yet even the New World did not change old habits or human nature. Once again, children became guilty of transgressions that required some formal intervention by authorities. Inevitably, the colonies returned to historical traditions as a basis for punishment in the New World. Compared with modern standards, these traditions seem harsh indeed.

OLD PUNISHMENTS REVISITED

The Puritans carried to the New World a belief in the importance of punishing children for theft, damage of private property, *blasphemy*, and disrespect to parents. There was no question that whipping was acceptable, but the debate centered on what kind of instrument to use, between what ages whipping was appropriate, and whether the skin should be bare or covered. Authorities also punished children by fining and *branding* (burning the hand) as well as by cutting off part or all of the offender's ear.

The Puritans were particularly harsh toward rebellious sons. The laws of Massachusetts and Connecticut used identical wording to specify that

> if any man have a stubborne and rebellious sonne of sufficient yeares and understanding, viz. [namely] six-teene years of age, which will not obey the voice of his father or the voice of his mother, that when they have chastened him will not hearken unto them; then may his father and mother, being his naturall parents, lay hold on him and bring him to the Magistrates as-sembled in Courte, and testifie unto them, that theire sonne is stubborne and rebellious and will not obey theire voice and Chastisement, but lives in sundry notorious Crimes, such a sonne shall bee put to death.

Even though children were rarely put to death for offenses, they were harshly punished. Nevertheless, the Renaissance idea that chil-dren are fundamentally different from adults continued to gain ground in American culture. In court rulings of the 18th and early 19th centuries, repeated evidence suggests that the judges felt that if other people, namely the child's parents or guardians, had fulfilled their own responsibilities, the child would never have come before the bench.

Sanders's book contains the record of one such case. In Boston Municipal Court on December 11, 1813, 3 boys between the ages of 13 and 16 were sentenced to 5 days of solitary confinement and 5 years of hard labor in the state prison for breaking into a store at night and stealing about $900 in bank bills. In reading their sentence, the judge pointed out that in any other part of the world, they would have been "hung between heaven and earth as unworthy of both."

Yet the judge was actually lenient because he had the "suspicion that some of the parents intrusted with your education are themselves too much to blame." He further instructed the culprits to read the Bible in prison and, in this place "appointed for the wicked," not to "select the worst of them for your companions."

REFUGE AT LAST

For a child, finding good role models would be difficult in a prison filled with hardened adults, and society was soon willing to act on that understanding. In an 1821 report on the penitentiary system in the United States, attorney Daniel Raymond recommended, "When a child or youth under 16 or 18 commits a crime, instead of inflicting that punishment provided for men, I would have them taken from their parents and placed under the care of some good master, who should instruct them, and teach them some mechanic art. Our temples of justice are too often profaned by arraigning children and youth, convicting and punishing them as men."

In 1825, New York built a House of Refuge for juvenile offenders that served as both a prison and a school, one of the first facilities designed especially for juvenile offenders. Soon more of these institutions began to emerge. They were constructed with great optimism, the fruit of the evolving idea that children are indeed different from adults, that they are born innocent and corrupted by society, and that society has the ability to restore them to morally upright, law-abiding, and socially constructive behavior.

In this environment, children who seriously misbehaved acquired a new name—juvenile delinquents. They would no longer be called criminals or be punished in the same way as an adult who violates the law. Until they were at least 16 years old, they would find some degree of shelter from the Old World consequences of destructive or rebellious acts. The next chapter will look at official treatment that would be accorded specifically to the juvenile delinquent.

CHAPTER 2

SEPARATE JUSTICE: THE JUVENILE COURTS

This 1877 woodcut shows a desperate mother pleading for the release of her son. Juvenile offenders were often sent directly to brutal prisons or reform schools.

Punishment was the only means Western society used to control crime prior to the 19th century. To modern minds, the cruelty of the punishment seems to far exceed the seriousness of the misdeed. If found guilty of stealing, children (as well as adults) could be hanged, thrown into prison for an indefinite time, or exiled to a penal colony in a foreign land for life. At the time, these punishments were thought to be justified, as a way to make the culprit pay society back for a wrongdoing. The concept of *rehabilitation*, of restoring the individual, whether a youth or an adult, to the biblical "path of righteousness" simply did not exist.

A CHANGE OF HEART

By the beginning of the 19th century, however, Americans had begun to search for alternative punishments that might also result in reform. A revolutionary concept began to catch on: The length of confinement should correspond to the seriousness of the criminal act. Reformers also believed that if prisoners were locked away from wicked influences in solitary cells—another innovation—they would repent their old habits and change their ways when they got out. Pennsylvania was

Attempts to reform delinquent children became popular in the mid-19th century in both the United States and Europe. These teachers at the North Market Hall School Mission in London are pictured with the youngsters they tried to help.

the first state to test this theory, passing a law in 1790 that led to the nation's first *penitentiary* (derived from the word *penitent*, meaning a person who repents for offenses).

American society was also beginning to embrace more progressive ideas about dealing with delinquent children. According to Empey, by the early 19th century most people already believed that children need special protection and care, such as a loving upbringing by their own parents, regular school attendance to learn moral principles as well as reading and writing, protection from evil influences, and the leeway to develop "at a leisurely pace rather than taking their place alongside adults at an early age."

The adults' growing awareness of children ensured that they would not simply be ignored. Their wild and disreputable behavior was no longer acceptable in an American society that placed a high value on morality, order, and private property. However, adults were not only worried about theft, violence, and destruction. As the nation grew, so did the problems within society. Concerned citizens became more aware of child abuse at home and in the workplace, *truancy* (staying out of school without permission), running away, begging, prostitution, idleness, disorderly conduct, and neglect by parents.

CHILDREN AND THE AUTHORITIES

In the 1850s, the first reform, training, and industrial schools—generally referred to as restraining facilities—emerged. By 1900, 36 states had separate restraining facilities for juvenile offenders. Originally, these institutions, built mainly before 1900, had a twofold purpose. They were developed as a way to remove troublesome children from society while keeping them separate from adult prisoners who were likely to influence youngsters even more negatively.

The courts also hoped that such facilities would help children find the structure and the moral guidance they needed to improve their ways. Yet these institutions were actually little better than prisons. Moreover, youngsters were often summarily dispatched to them—without a formal trial—by the courts, the police, their parents, or their guardians.

In this 1908 photograph by Lewis Hines, the police are enforcing early child labor laws, making certain that youngsters who have applied for working papers meet size requirements.

When these types of facilities were not available, children were sent to adult jails and prisons for every sort of offense, from general unruliness to assault with a deadly weapon.

AN INSTITUTIONAL PARENT

A medieval English doctrine called *parens patriae* influenced this negative attitude toward young people. Basically, it affirmed the British crown's right to intrude in family relations when a child's welfare was at issue. Similarly, the state governments in America affirmed their rights to stand as guardian of any and all minors. Yet this authority was often exercised too arbitrarily—to the point that restraining facilities became overcrowded.

One well-known example is the *People v. Turner*, a case tried in Illinois in 1870. A young boy named Daniel O'Connell was arrested for a minor criminal offense and committed to a Chicago reform school for an indefinite period of time. He was arrested under a law passed in 1867 that authorized apprehension of "any boy or girl, within the ages of 6 and 16 years who . . . is a vagrant, or is destitute of proper parental care, or is growing up in mendicancy [begging], ignorance, idleness or vice." Although the legal system had this view of Daniel, his father disagreed.

Mr. O'Connell filed suit to get Daniel out of reform school, and the court ultimately released him, maintaining in its final statement that "the disability of minors does not make slaves or criminals of them. The principle of the absorption of the child in, and its complete subjection to the despotism of, the State, is wholly inadmissible in the modern civilized world." According to Steven L. Schlossman in his book, *Love and the American Delinquent*, the ruling is notable not only for its enlightenment but also for the way it was profoundly ignored.

Late in the 19th century, reformers were becoming more and more critical of how the juvenile restraining facilities worked. Homer Folks, head of the Pennsylvania Children's Aid Society, expressed a popular viewpoint in an 1891 speech. He was concerned that parents found it easy to abandon their responsibilities and to commit their children without good reason because there were now so many such institutions. He observed that the stigma attached to having spent time in a reform school was almost as damaging as a prison record, and a long sentence could make it impossible for a young person to readapt to normal life. Even the best facilities could not provide enough individual treatment, Folks pointed out, so that many of the anticipated benefits from constructive guidance had no effect.

LEGAL LENIENCY

Growing disenchantment with existing institutions designed to deal with unmanageable youth led to swift acceptance of the idea of a juvenile court. In 1870, Boston began holding separate hearings for offenders under age 16, and New York City soon followed suit. In 1899, Illinois became the first state to establish a juvenile court system. Other states quickly did the same.

Separating young people from hardened criminals was the driving conviction behind the establishment of juvenile courts. Sponsors of the juvenile court system did not want young people associating with adult criminals in *penal* (punishment) institutions. In fact, they did not want them in such facilities at all. One of the main goals of the juvenile court system was to keep young offenders out of institutions. This system promoted the term *juvenile delinquent* in order to distinguish between an adult criminal and a misbehaving child who may or may not be guilty of criminal conduct.

According to James S. Coleman, writing on the youth's transition to adulthood, the juvenile court system introduced an entirely new goal. Its purpose was to rehabilitate the child rather than to punish him or her. The rights of children were redefined in terms of "protecting them

In the 20th century, authorities made more attempts to rehabilitate, rather than simply imprison, juveniles. Teaching job skills is one of the ideals behind modern reform schools.

from parental neglect and abuse, immorality, excessive and dangerous work, and ensuring that they attended school in order to prepare themselves for adulthood."

At the same time that the juvenile court system sought to protect young people from threatening family situations, it also tried to achieve rehabilitation by working with the family. According to Schlossman, the court's role and function emerged from the basic belief that no institution "could replace the affectional ties between most natural parents and their offspring." In its efforts to focus on the home as the place where a child could be saved, the courts relied on the idea of *probation*, wherein an individual can be released and return home if he or she promises to maintain good behavior.

PROCEDURES OF THE COURT

Originally, the juvenile court system was not intended as the first place an identified problem child would go. Rather, the court was to remain in the background while its *probation officers* (appointed officials who supervise and report on an offender's behavior) tried to help parents fulfill their responsibilities.

Probation Officers

The idea of a probation officer for children originated in the 1840s when a shoemaker in Boston, John Augustus, convinced officials to let him work with first offenders and find them foster homes when necessary. Yet Augustus's idea was not officially incorporated into the legal system until Massachusetts passed the first probation law— originally for adults—in 1878. Later, when the first juvenile court systems were established, they made probation officers an integral part of their structure.

These early probation officers were intended to serve as a kind of tutor to the entire family, teaching children and parents about their responsibilities toward one another. An officer was also expected to preach to the family about moral and religious ideals, inform them about child care and home economics, and discipline youngsters who shirked their schoolwork.

The officer's advice and efforts to connect the family with available community services sometimes made a trip to court unnecessary. If, however, a probation officer felt that the services he or she could provide were not adequate to the situation, the officer could bring the child and family to juvenile court.

Inside the Courts

Once the probation officer decided that a situation needed to be resolved in court, the court dealt with the case using its established structure. This basic structure, including the assistance of probation officers, is still in use today. It requires that a case pass through a series of three basic steps—*intake*, *adjudication*, and *disposition*—before a juvenile is sentenced.

Before facing a hearing, juveniles are read a statement of formal charges. These teens, ages 15 and 16, were charged with first-degree murder of a 14 year old. The incident occurred when a group of boys with air rifles shot at the 2 suspects, who fired back with .22-caliber rifles.

Intake

Intake is the process wherein the child's case enters the juvenile court system. An official of the court collects pertinent information and then decides whether or not the child's case should go through the official legal process. In many first-offense and less serious cases, the officer dismisses the case. For more serious offenses, the officer passes the case on to the court system, along with observations that may help the judge choose the court's strategy.

When a juvenile's case is not dismissed, the next step usually occurs within the same day. This requires the city's legal department to file a formal *petition*, a statement of charges, which presents the case against the child. The department then sets a date for a *hearing*, an informal sort of trial. If the judge decides that the juvenile can be released to his or her family, a hearing is scheduled for a later date. If the charges are serious, the child may be *detained*—sent to a temporary residence facility for young offenders.

Adjudication

Adjudication is the process whereby a judge determines for which category of offense the individual should be tried. For example, serious offenders may be waived to criminal court and tried as adults. Less serious cases go directly to a *fact-finding hearing*, an inquiry that is less formal than a trial but involves a lawyer to represent the juvenile. (Although hearings are similar to trials, the court system avoids using the word *trial* in reference to juveniles.)

In more serious cases, the juvenile first undergoes a *probable-cause hearing*, wherein he or she is represented by a lawyer, and a judge determines whether there is probable cause to believe the juvenile committed the act for which he or she has been charged. If the court finds probable cause, the case proceeds to a fact-finding hearing.

If a child is found guilty at the fact-finding hearing, the case is referred to a *dispositional hearing*, a more formal court proceeding that includes sentencing. This hearing is scheduled to occur within 8 weeks, or within 20 days for juveniles who have been detained. (These time periods may vary from state to state.)

Disposition

Disposition is the process wherein the judge determines what will be done with the child, similar to sentencing in an adult trial. The judge may still decide to dismiss the case, which would allow the juvenile's

The most serious juvenile offenses may be tried in adult courts. The 1986 Howard Beach trial in New York involved a racially motivated attack of a black man by white youths. John Lester, 17, was convicted of manslaughter and sentenced to prison for 10 to 30 years.

court record to be sealed as a right of privacy. If the judge does not dismiss the case at this point, he or she must determine whether a child is neglected and needs supervision or a different life-style than his or her family provides. In some cases, the judge may decide that a youngster's behavior is truly uncontrollable and needs restraint.

Once the judge makes this decision, he or she may choose from several options. A juvenile may be discharged on the condition that he or she will be supervised by a court official, placed on probation and referred to the care of a social agency, placed in a community-based residence, or placed in a long-term institution for juveniles. A judge usually opts for the less severe levels of sentencing before sending a young person to a juvenile institution.

THE MODERN COURT'S CASELOAD

Juvenile court cases are divided into two general categories: *status offenses* and *delinquency offenses*. A status offense is an act or conduct that is an offense only when committed by a juvenile. That is, if an adult performed the action, he or she would not be committing an offense. These actions include truancy, underage drinking, or running away from home.

A delinquency offense is an act committed by a juvenile for which an adult would be prosecuted in criminal court. These include *property offenses*, such as shoplifting, burglary, or trespassing; *offenses against the public order*, such as disorderly conduct, public drunkenness, contempt of court, or escape from an institution; *person offenses*, such as robbery or aggravated or simple assault; and *drug violations*, such as possession or sale of a controlled substance.

Juvenile court statistics from the U.S. Department of Justice show that out of a total of 1,145,000 cases handled in 1987, about 93% were for delinquency offenses. This represents approximately 44.4 violations for every 1,000 juveniles. Most of these cases (59%) were property offenses; 19% were offenses against the public order; 16% were person offenses; and 6% were drug violations. In the same year, a total of 81,000 status offenses were recorded. Among these, 31% were attributable to liquor-law violations, 27% to truancy, 17% to ungovernability, 17% to running away from home, and 8% to miscellaneous causes.

In each of these cases the juvenile court has a variety of options: (1) to dismiss the case; (2) to put the juvenile on probation; (3) to place him or her in the custody of relatives, a foster family, or a child-care agency; (4) to make him or her pay a fine or restitution; or (5) to commit him or her to an institution. Delinquency offenses can also be referred to a criminal court, where the juvenile is then tried as an adult.

The 1987 statistics show that about 60% of juveniles whose cases are disposed of by the court are put on probation. Between 20% and 30% of young offenders are placed out of their own homes, depending on whether they are charged with status or delinquency offenses. Approximately half of the delinquency cases brought to court are *handled formally*, meaning that the court files a petition and schedules a hearing. One-fifth of those cases are ultimately dismissed.

The juvenile court system is facing numerous criticisms. One is that the rising rate of offenses indicates that juvenile courts are not dealing effectively with serious juvenile crime. Another is that the courts are not dealing fairly with the juveniles who get caught in the system. These problems will be discussed more fully in the next chapter.

CHAPTER 3

THE JUVENILE COURT ON TRIAL

Juvenile arrests often lie in a police officer's hands. When offenses are not severe enough to charge the child, officers may release a youngster with a warning.

In its early days, the juvenile court's primary aim was rehabilitation, not punishment. Ideally, the court's decisions would be shaped by each individual's needs, not the nature of the offense. Everyone would be concerned first and foremost with the youth's well-being, making the presence of attorneys and legal restraints unnecessary. Supporters hoped that the kind and just processes of the juvenile court system would turn a troubled youth into a stable and upstanding member of society.

Yet these high goals were hard to achieve in a system that would work throughout the entire country. By 1920, all but three states had juvenile court laws. (In 1950, Wyoming became the last state to join the movement.) But the way juveniles were treated varied radically from court to court and state to state. The attitudes of the judges who served in different courts were inconsistent, as was the number of probation officers and juvenile institutions that states would support. The number of cases in which courts acted in an arbitrary and unreasonable fashion prompted a growing concern about the system's potential for abuse of individual rights.

It was inevitable that society would become disillusioned with the juvenile court system, simply because everyone had expected so much from it. Ted Rubin, a former judge of the Denver juvenile court, described the situation as follows:

> This court is a far more complex instrument than outsiders imagine. It is law, and it is social work; it is control, and it is help; it is the good parent and, also, the stern parent; it is both formal and informal. It is concerned not only with the delinquent, but also with the battered child, the runaway, and many others. . . . The juvenile court has been all things to all people.

CONSTITUTIONAL RIGHTS FOR CHILDREN

Although the creation of juvenile courts spanned half a century, the flaws in the system began to appear as early as the system itself did. In a study of 16 juvenile cases conducted in Milwaukee in the early 20th century, Schlossman found numerous abuses of the early juvenile court. He pointed out that, contrary to the friendly and compassionate communications that might have been expected, "judges and probation officers relied mainly on fear, threats, and short-term imprisonment to render children malleable and 'cooperative.'"

Schlossman also found that the courts tended to press their authority to the limit. Judges, probation officers, and district attorneys asked every form of improper question and gave weight to both hearsay and circumstantial evidence. Their inquiries into the reasons for the children's problems, which could have led to valuable insights into their needs, were often superficial. These court officials also placed children in *double jeopardy*, meaning that during a trial they would bring up previous charges for which the child had already been tried. At other times, these officials would solicit confessions to get them and their parents into even more serious trouble.

Kent v. U.S.

Finally, processes such as these were challenged in the U.S. Supreme Court. In two celebrated cases, the Court voiced weighty criticisms and imposed new guidelines for the juvenile system. The first such ruling, for *Kent v. U.S.*, came in 1966. It involved a 14-year-old boy named Morris Kent who was arrested in Washington, D.C., for a rape and robbery. Although the boy admitted to the crime, the Supreme Court eventually dismissed the case on grounds of procedural irregularity. That is, the boy had been tried in violation of *due process*, rights ensuring that legal proceedings are carried out according to established rules.

The 1966 Supreme Court made a landmark decision entitling juveniles to the same due process rights as adults. Although each state had established its own juvenile court system by 1950, the disparities among them eventually required the Supreme Court to protect children's constitutional rights.

Guns in Young Hands

One of the most frightening aspects of recent juvenile life is the rising number of teenage deaths caused by guns. Between 1984 and 1988, the firearm death rate for 15 to 19 year olds increased by an astonishing 43%. Gun homicides took the life of 1,641 teenagers in 1988, compared with 1,022 in 1984, according to the National Center for Health Statistics.

Firearm murders committed by offenders under the age of 18 more than doubled within a 5-year period. According to the National Crime Analysis Program at Northeastern University, this age-group was responsible for 444 homicides in 1984, 615 in 1987, and 952 in 1989. This growing rate of juvenile homicide has spurred increasing concern about juvenile crime.

Even when youngsters do not use their weapons to kill, guns are a source of trouble. The number of arrests for weapons violations among juveniles age 17 and under increased from 19,649 in 1976 to 31,577 in 1989. One study in a Florida school reported that 86% of the guns confiscated from students came from the students' own home. Many other juveniles acquire guns through theft. Later, the weapons are sold or rented to teenagers who are untrained in the proper use of firearms. A survey of 11,000 students in 20 states showed that 41% of the boys felt they could obtain a handgun if they wanted to.

Young people carry guns for a variety of reasons. Gang members, for example, use guns to protect themselves and to create a tough image. Still others believe that they must prove they are willing to use a gun—a type of thinking that often leads to both the random shootings into crowds and the drive-by shootings that mark gang rivalry.

Even nongang members may carry a gun in an attempt to gain respect or impress their peers. Unfortunately, an inexperienced teenager may be tempted to use a gun at random. For example, one 17-year-old boy in Los Angeles admitted to killing someone while under the influence of *PCP*, a drug that may cause a user to suddenly become violent. One estimate suggests that 20% to 25% of the teenagers who shoot someone are high on drugs at the time; other studies claim that the rate is much higher.

Because so many teenagers now have guns, others may feel a pressure to carry one for self-defense. According to the National School Safety Center, approximately 135,000 students carried guns to school in 1987. Many young people are becoming afraid to attend schools in which gun violence has increased. A recent survey taken throughout Illinois high schools reported that 1 in 12 students admitted to feeling so fearful that he or she missed school. Nationwide, in the 4 academic years preceding 1991, at least 71 people were killed with guns at school, and 201 were badly wounded.

Communities are responding in a variety of ways. One program in Dade County, Florida, takes videos, books, and role-playing into the classrooms to show the disadvantages of gun use. Boston, Massachusetts, maintains a rigorous program for students caught with a weapon: It sends them to a counseling center for a 10-day program of psychological and educational assessment tests. The program then shows the youngsters alternative ways to avoid violence. Out of 1,000 participants, only 5% have needed to return for further treatment.

Still other people look for ways to stop the spread of guns at their source. Some suggest reducing the number of available guns by establishing stricter gun control laws. Others recommend that guns be manufactured with a combination lock so that only the person who purchases and owns the gun would be able to pull the trigger.

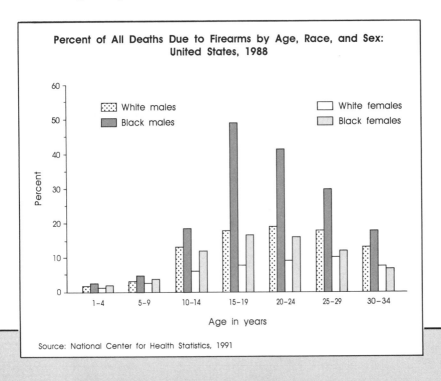

Percent of All Deaths Due to Firearms by Age, Race, and Sex: United States, 1988

Source: National Center for Health Statistics, 1991

Several due process rights had been violated in the Kent case: The boy's parents had not been notified of his arrest; he had been interrogated without being informed of his rights to remain silent or to have a lawyer present; he had been detained without a probable-cause hearing; and police had matched his fingerprints from previous files, a violation of confidentiality. In *Kent v. U.S.*, the Court stated that "while there can be no doubt of the original laudable purpose of juvenile courts . . . there may be grounds for concern that the child receives the worst of both worlds: that he gets neither the protection accorded adults nor the solicitous care and regenerative treatment postulated for children."

In re Gault

The *In re Gault* case, tried in 1967, provides another example of the way in which juvenile courts deprived children of the constitutional rights enjoyed by adults. In this instance, a 15-year-old Arizona boy named Gerald Gault was charged with making an obscene phone call to his neighbor. The authorities arrested Gerald and put him in a *detention center*, a temporary residence for juveniles awaiting disposition by the court. Gerald's parents never received notification of the charges filed against him.

Gerald was sentenced to remain in a state institution for 6 years, because state law allowed him to be held until he was 21 years old. If he had been at least 18 years old, Gerald would have been tried as an adult and imprisoned in jail for no more than 2 months or fined between $5 and $50.

The Supreme Court ruled that the state of Arizona was depriving children of procedural safeguards guaranteed by the Constitution. It held that children in juvenile court are entitled to certain due process guarantees that had been omitted in Gerald's case. Both the parents and the child must be given notice of the charges against the child and time to prepare a defense. Children are also entitled to representation by an attorney. The Court asserted that "neither the Fourteenth Amendment nor the Bill of Rights is for adults alone."

A PRESIDENTIAL COMMISSION

In the 1960s, people became further disillusioned with the juvenile court system due to rising crime rates among young people. Traditional views of teenagers also began to change when students openly rebelled in protest movements, including *sit-ins* and *love-ins*. In 1965, President Lyndon B. Johnson established the Commission on Law Enforcement and the Administration of Justice to take stock of rising crime rates and to recommend reforms.

The commission published a report in 1967 that indicted the juvenile court system for ineffectiveness, saying that it had not "succeeded significantly in rehabilitating delinquent youth, in reducing or even stemming the tide of juvenile criminality, or in bringing justice and compassion to the child offender." The report reflected a greater faith in the community to solve youth problems than the courts, whose interference it considered both stigmatizing and destructive.

The commission recommended that (1) juveniles not be prosecuted for behavior that would not be prosecuted in an adult; (2) those who have committed less serious offenses be given warnings in order to avoid court processing or diverting the offending youths into community-run agencies; (3) procedures to protect a youth's constitutional rights be meticulously observed; and (4) correctional efforts be moved from reform, training, and industrial institutions to community settings, such as foster homes.

POLICE INVOLVEMENT WITH JUVENILE DELINQUENTS

The court's failings are intertwined with the channel through which most of its referrals come—the police. Anyone can file a petition that brings the court's attention to juvenile behavior within its jurisdiction. Yet it is the police who respond to these complaints. In 1987 about 84% of all delinquency cases were referred to courts by the police.

When juveniles are apprehended, the police have several options. They can (1) take juveniles to the station house and release them to their parents; (2) refer them to the juvenile bureau of the department, if they have one; (3) refer them to a welfare agency; or (4) refer them directly to a juvenile court.

According to Empey, the police handle most cases themselves: They typically release about half the juveniles they arrest with a simple warning. The police are often lenient because they believe the juvenile court system is overly lenient. In general, Empey claims, many police officers dislike working with juveniles, preferring to be backed by a more severe system of justice than a "soft-headed rehabilitative system" that is unequal to the challenge of serious crime.

At least partially as a result of these attitudes, the number of police referrals to juvenile court may misrepresent the extent of the country's delinquency problem. In his book, *Saving Our Kids from Delinquency,*

These police officers are searching gang members for weapons. Statistics showing that police are more inclined to arrest nonwhites than whites are due in part to the large number of minority gangs. The impoverished conditions of ghettos make gang membership attractive to many minority youths.

Drugs, and Despair, Falcon Baker explains that criminologists believe that far more juveniles commit delinquent acts than are ever reported. In fact, dozens of studies conducted over the last 40 years offer astonishingly high estimates of delinquency: At least 95% of American young people have committed acts for which they could have been arrested and taken to juvenile court. Yet a distinct pattern differentiates youths who are actually arrested from those who are not.

Studies suggest that a young person's race affects the arrest rate. Baker cites the National Youth Survey, an ongoing study of delinquent behavior performed by the University of Colorado Institute of Behavioral Science. The survey of 11-through-17-year-old youths indicates that a young black person is twice as likely to be arrested as a young white person for committing an equivalent crime. For minor offenses the probability is seven times as great.

Because most arrests result from citizen complaints, police action probably reflects society's attitudes in general. Apparently, people expect to see more delinquent behavior among poor, disadvantaged, and minority groups, and police action confirms those expectations. In addition, arrest patterns may also reflect the high rate of minority youths involved in *gangs*, groups of people who work together, often for antisocial or unlawful purposes.

THE CASE AGAINST THE JUVENILE COURTS

In recent years, critics of the juvenile court system have accused it of (1) failing to protect society from youthful criminals, (2) failing to be compassionate, (3) failing to be just, and (4) doing more harm than good. Recent cases and statistics substantiate these accusations.

Failing to Protect Society

Justice department statistics show that violent crimes committed by juveniles increased 22% between 1988 and 1989, with rape increasing 14%. Another example is the January 1989 *Juvenile Justice Bulletin* report on a 12-state survey of criminal law violations in 1984. The report shows that more than two-thirds of the juveniles apprehended for violent offenses, including homicide (murder), violent sex offenses, robbery, and aggravated assault (a violent attack with an intent to commit a crime), were released or put on probation. Only slightly more than a third of juveniles charged with homicide were transferred to adult criminal court for trial.

Additionally, a *New York Times* investigative reporter discovered in 1982 that just slightly more than 1 out of every 100 New York youths arrested for muggings, beatings, rape, and murder ended up in a correctional institution. A similar report in Chicago showed that a delinquent boy has to be arrested an average of 13.5 times before the court will take any action more restrictive than mere probation.

Even when the courts are empowered to act more severely, there is apparently some reluctance to do so. In 1978, the New York legislature

Yusef Salaam, 16, was implicated in the famous 1990 case of a group of youths who beat and raped a female jogger in New York's Central Park. The incident drew attention to the extent of violence among youths, a sign that the present justice system does not prevent juvenile crime.

passed a law permitting district attorneys to try as adults juveniles over the age of 12 who commit violent crimes. But in the 10 years since the law was passed, only 14% of these serious offenders served time in a correctional institution, and only 4% received sentences longer than those permitted prior to the 1978 law.

The adult criminal world understands and takes advantage of this lenience toward youthful offenders. To illustrate this, Baker uses the comments of a 21-year-old former drug hustler about the increased employment of juveniles by drug pushers. "The pushers get the young kids to hold the drugs," the hustler explains, "'cause if they get arrested they just go to children's court. The judge spanks their hands and tells them, 'Go home. Don't do that no more.'"

On Compassion and Justice

Although some critics of the juvenile court system feel it is too lenient with lawbreakers, others criticize it for being overly harsh. In 1974, the 3,000 members of the National Council of Jewish Women spent a year surveying the juvenile justice system in 30 states and published their findings in a book entitled *Children Without Justice*. In it they claim that many cases are tried too quickly to guarantee a fair trial: In more than half of the cases, juvenile hearings lasted less than 15 minutes. They also report that children undergo overly harsh treatment in court, that rehabilitation programs are inadequate, and that many juvenile correctional institutions allow terrible living conditions to go unchanged.

The 1984 case of *Gary v. Hegstrom* supported these assertions of squalid conditions when describing the MacLaren School for Boys. U.S. District Court judge James Burns reported, "The cells were dirty and unsanitary. Students testified that the cells were infested with silverfish, cockroaches, flies and spiders, as well as body lice, and that the walls were covered with food, spit, blood, toilet paper and feces." The court also found that physical restraints such as handcuffs and leg irons substituted for psychological services and educational programs.

Other sources underscore discrimination throughout the juvenile justice system as a whole. For instance, 1987 juvenile court statistics indicate that 50% of the cases involving nonwhite juveniles were handled formally, compared with 42% of the cases involving white juveniles. Nonwhites were more than twice as likely to be detained if a drug-law violation was involved. Nonwhites were slightly less likely (56%, compared with 58%) to be placed on formal probation.

The prison system often does not help offenders change their old life-style and bad habits. These Florida inmates are entering a Boot Camp program as an alternative to prison. Those who do not succeed leave their hats on the fence when they leave for prison—a warning to others who might fail.

This pattern of racial bias continues when juveniles are taken to court. Records show that 27% of nonwhites were put into detention centers, compared with 17% of whites. Nonwhites were also more likely than whites (2.6% versus 1.8%) to be waived to criminal court, and to be placed out of their homes (33%, compared with 28%).

More Harm Than Good

Can the juvenile court system actually harm the young people it is designed to help? A 1973 study directed by Martin Gold at the University of Michigan Institute for Social Research provides some interesting statistics to answer this question. The institute took samples of teenagers from the 48 contiguous states: Half of them had committed offenses but escaped prosecution; the other half were arrested for similar offenses.

The study found that the young people who had been arrested were twice as likely to commit additional criminal acts. It seems that apprehended juveniles are treated by society, police, and the court system in a way that encourages them to become progressively more antisocial and ultimately criminal in their behavior. When children enter the justice system they are often treated as though they are already criminals, an attitude that greatly damages their self-esteem. Once they find themselves among other offenders, they begin to learn, and eventually to imitate, worse types of behavior.

Massachusetts provides another example of the negative impact of the juvenile court system. As commissioner of the Department of Youth Services in 1972, Jerome Miller closed all of its large training schools when his reform efforts failed. But juvenile crime did not soar; instead it declined. However, the training schools were eventually reopened in 1975, when the state needed a place to confine severe youth offenders, such as rapists, murderers, and dangerous schizophrenics.

Peter Edelman, former director of the New York State Division for Youth, has stated that juveniles who are kept in large institutions, at a cost of $23,900 per child per year, have a 65% rate of rearrest. Other estimates place the cost of imprisonment between $25,000 and $50,000 per person per year—more than the annual tuition at some of the nation's best colleges.

THE CURRENT ATTITUDE

As far as juvenile delinquents are concerned, some critics feel they would be better off if the authorities did not try so hard to help. Milton Leuger, head of the federal Office of Juvenile Justice and Delinquency Prevention, expresses an increasingly popular viewpoint: "With the exception of a relatively few youths, it is probably better for all concerned if young delinquents were not detected, apprehended, or institutionalized. Too many of them get worse in our care."

Yet rather than throw up its hands in despair, society is trying to find new ways of preventing and responding to delinquency. This process involves searching for its causes. Why is it, for example, that certain children become juvenile delinquents and others do not, even when they come from the same family, neighborhood, ethnic group, or income level? This question, which has troubled scholars for generations, will be addressed in the next chapter.

CHAPTER 4

CAUSES OF DELINQUENCY

This Jacob Riis photograph documents three boys in an 1890s New York City tenement district, an early form of today's ghettos. Experts propose that environment, rather than inborn traits, determines whether a child becomes delinquent.

If there were a way to identify in early childhood those individuals who would become delinquents, these children could immediately be given the support and guidance to direct them onto more constructive paths. Of course, no such indicator exists. Over the years, however, a number of theories have shaped society's understanding of the complex causes of juvenile delinquency.

BORN DELINQUENTS?

In the late 19th century, a psychiatrist named Cesare Lombroso proposed that all criminals had certain physical characteristics in common. He described these features as large jaws, high cheekbones, and protruding ears. Lombroso's supporters extended this theory to juvenile delinquents, adding that they also sport a husky, muscular build. This idea lost credibility when people realized that this physique is common in all competitive areas, such as sports, the military, and business.

Other theories suggested that the tendency toward criminality is a biologically inherited trait. Researchers studied patterns across several generations within families but could not find a solid pattern of criminal history. Numerous studies of twins showed some possibility that criminal tendencies could be *genetic*, or biologically inherited. For example, identical twins (who have the exact same genes) are more likely to share delinquent behavior than are fraternal twins (whose genes are different). This does not mean, however, that delinquency is inevitable in certain individuals or racial groups.

But according to Donald J. Shoemaker, writing in his book, *Theories of Delinquency*, none of the research in this area has yet presented conclusive evidence of a biological predisposition toward criminal behavior. He suggests that delinquent behavior is more likely to be learned within the family than to be inherited biologically; in fact, modern psychologists no longer examine the idea that delinquents are produced from "degenerate stock."

Similarly, juvenile delinquency is predominantly a problem within the male population. Department of Justice figures indicate that males commit about four times as many delinquency offenses and about seven times as many violent crimes as do females. However, this does not mean that males are genetically inclined to become criminals. Rather, their social environments require a different sort of behavior than that expected of females.

THE ROLE OF ENVIRONMENT

The theory that environmental factors cause juvenile delinquency has been popular in the United States and Europe since the 19th century. According to Englishman Paul Morris, a sociologist who studies prisons, the three most influential factors are poverty, ignorance, and population density.

These factors generally occur in inner-city environments, where juvenile delinquency is known to thrive. Research conducted over the past 60 years indicates that delinquency rates decline as one moves

The Tremont section of Cleveland, Ohio, was a thriving community that dwindled with the Industrial Revolution. Similar areas share three important factors thought to increase delinquency rates—poverty, ignorance, and overcrowding.

farther from the inner city. The highest rates are typically found in declining industrial areas; the lowest occur in primarily residential areas.

Recent statistics show an increasing number of young people living in poverty. According to U.S. government figures from 1987, a family of 4 is living in poverty if their annual income is $11,603 or less. Thus, in 1987, 20.4% of all Americans under the age of 18 were living in poverty, compared with 17.9% in 1980. Between 1980 and 1987, the number of impoverished young people grew from 11 million to 13 million. The connection between rising rates of juvenile poverty and crime is apparent.

When describing juvenile delinquents, Baker focuses on America's *underclass*, a social class having the lowest status in society. In America, the underclass is typically a *ghetto* culture. Ghettos are areas within a city where minority groups tend to live, often due to social or economic pressure. In these neighborhoods, unemployment, crime, and drug addiction are common problems. Many people must depend on welfare to survive.

Inner-city teenagers experience a different life-style than their suburban or rural counterparts do: Pregnant, unmarried teens are the norm, as are school dropouts and illiterates. Many of these young people believe that their only chance of escape is through drug use and that their only opportunity to make money is through drug dealing. These values usually do not make sense to many Americans who have experienced healthier and happier upbringings.

Baker claims that the value systems in these ghettos "have spawned a major portion of the most serious and violent juvenile crime in America." He points to a 1988 Department of Justice survey of inmates in state-operated institutions. Baker believes that the statistics on inmates parallel the characteristics of ghetto residents:

- Three-fourths grew up with only one parent.
- Two-thirds are from minority groups.
- More than half report that at least one close family member has been institutionalized.

- Well over half dropped out of school long before entering high school.

- More than 60% have used drugs regularly, about half of whom began before the age of 12.

THE IMPORTANCE OF FAMILY

Despite the juvenile court system's efforts to act as an institutional parent, society still views the family as the key to America's juvenile delinquency problem. When an individual in a ghetto rises above his or her disadvantages to become a productive citizen, this difference is often due to the values and support provided by the individual's family.

A supportive family situation does not require that both parents be present. More essential is that a parent treat a child with love, affection, respect, and fair discipline.

By the same token, youngsters who get involved in crime often lack this solid background.

Yet the successful family requires something other than the strong discipline that many people might expect. A 1958 study reported by F. Ivan Nye in his book *Family Relationships and Delinquent Behavior* showed that fewer cases of delinquency occurred among adolescents whose parents treated them with love and respect. Having parents who continually nagged or scolded their children or who rigidly required them to behave well before giving them affection or approval was thought to provoke delinquent behavior.

Though juvenile delinquents frequently come from single-parent homes broken by divorce, desertion, or death, this loss may be less important than other factors that affect behavior. Studies conducted by Sheldon and Eleanor Glueck at Harvard in the 1950s indicate that the quality of surviving relationships is more important than whether one parent is absent. The Gluecks defined family factors that create a more positive upbringing: dependable and fair supervision by the father or mother, appropriate affection of the father or mother for the child, and the closeness of the family.

The Value of Respect

In his well-known book *Causes of Delinquency*, Travis Hirschi describes characteristics that reduce the potential for delinquent behavior. First, he contends that children who are strongly attached to their parents are more likely to follow society's norms and respect others, especially authority figures.

In addition to learning respect for authority, Hirschi believes the qualities of commitment, involvement, and respect are equally important. For example, a child who has committed him- or herself to accomplishing a long-term goal, such as getting an education or pursuing a career, will find delinquent behavior unappealing and counterproductive. Similarly, involvement in activities such as sports, clubs, hobbies, or studies helps to fill the idle time when young people often get into trouble.

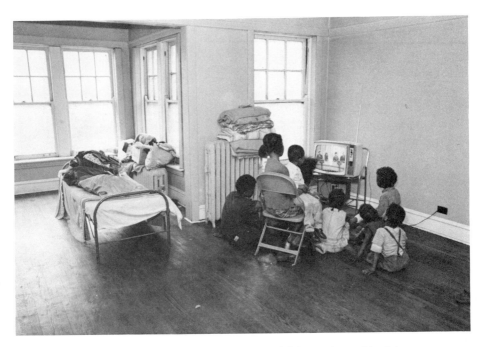

Children with a special interest or project establish goals and build self-esteem. In contrast, too much idle time may increase a young person's opportunities to get into trouble.

The final quality that Hirschi stresses is a belief in the importance of the law. A person without a conscience usually does not feel guilt or regret when he or she breaks the law, and someone who has been raised to feel contempt for the law may deliberately break it out of anger or rebelliousness. But a young person who respects the value of the law is less likely to violate it.

Child Abuse

A relationship with a parent or similarly concerned adult is probably the most important aspect in shaping a youngster's respect for authority. Yet a parental relationship can have a devastating effect if the adult does not influence the child in a positive way. Surveys

Is TV Responsible for Violence?

By the time most American children complete high school, they will have witnessed 18,000 murders plus a wide assortment of assaults, bombings, burglaries, and tortures—all of them on TV. According to the Nielsen Index, the organization that monitors nationwide viewing habits, children between the ages of 2 and 12 typically watch 25 hours of TV each week. Upon graduation from high school they will have watched 15,000 hours of TV, compared with spending 11,000 hours in class.

There is no doubt that children learn from television. Indeed, TV has given many preschoolers a jump on kindergarten because of educational shows such as "Sesame Street" and "Mr. Rogers' Neighborhood." Yet a growing number of parents, teachers, psychologists, and psychiatrists are concerned that the boob tube has also led to rising rates of aggression and violence among young people.

In its influential 1982 study, the National Institute of Mental Health (NIMH) reported numerous findings that violence on TV "leads to aggressive behavior by children and teenagers." A study conducted by L. D. Eron at the University of Illinois found that children who are most influenced by TV are those who identify closely with characters and believe the programs to be realistic. Eron found that these attitudes toward television are commonly shared by children who were rated by their peers as being highly aggressive.

Various studies have also criticized television's effect on viewers' perceptions of reality. According to a well-known study by George Gerbner at the University of Pennsylvania, heavy TV watchers believe the world to be much more violent than those who watch less TV. Not surprisingly, TV crimes occur about 10 times as often as they do in real life, according to Victor Strasburger, a professor of pediatrics at Yale University.

Television's ability to shape perception by making fictional events seem real can have a particularly strong effect on young children, especially as they flip from one thrilling adventure to another without waiting to learn a program's outcome. Thus, youngsters may see characters getting what they want through violence without viewing an ending that carries an important message: Crime does not pay. According to the NIMH study, even when they watch an entire episode, younger children are often unable to connect a program's moral conclusion with the preceding events.

Some critics of television blame the increasing rate of violent crime in real life on a corresponding increase on TV. Psychiatrist Thomas Radecki, chairman of the National Coalition on Television Violence, points out that only 8% of prime-time programming in the early 1950s focused on violence. In recent decades, he says, that percentage has increased to between 30% and 55% each year. Radecki links the rise in prime-time violence to the increasing rate of crime.

On the other side of the TV violence debate, many experts argue that much of the research linking aggressive behavior to TV violence is inaccurate. They point out that research is likely to be biased because it is difficult to prove that TV is the only factor that causes aggression. Some defenders of TV violence refer to a 1971 study showing that viewers who watched only nonviolent programs were actually more aggressive than those who watched only violent programs for the same amount of time.

Many people who defend TV violence are simply trying to protect the First Amendment right to freedom of expression. Proponents of this view claim that limiting violence on television is tantamount to censorship. Instead, they recommend that parents guide their children's viewing habits and suggest they discuss the situations and values that arise when violence appears in the mass media. In this way, they say, children can learn how to face society's inevitable violence with an informed and prepared attitude.

consistently indicate that between 60% and 80% of runaways leave home due to some form of abuse. Child abuse is a destructive habit, passed from one generation to the next. (Most parents who abuse their children were themselves abused as children.)

Such mistreatment also leads to more serious forms of delinquency than merely running away. Karl Menninger, the venerated psychiatrist of the Menninger Clinic who worked toward criminal justice for 50 years, observed, "Nearly every inmate I ever interviewed at length had been brutally beaten as a child by his father or stepfather or other power figure. . . . Everything we call crime is a rather stupid, mismanaged, pitiful struggle by angry kids to get revenge in the most evil way they can."

Child abuse, which has increased drastically in recent years, is thought to be responsible for many delinquency problems. Between 60% and 80% of runaways leave home because of abuse. Many inmates express intense anger about having suffered mistreatment as children.

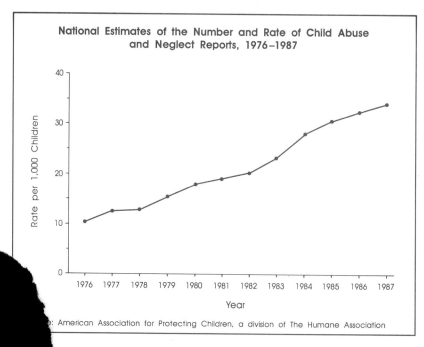

National Estimates of the Number and Rate of Child Abuse and Neglect Reports, 1976–1987

Rate per 1,000 Children

Year

Source: American Association for Protecting Children, a division of The Humane Association

THE IMPORTANCE OF SOCIAL ATTACHMENTS

One of the most important factors in the prevention of delinquent behavior is simply some kind of anchor for the child—whether it is a family, an individual (such as a teacher or a friend), an activity, or an institution that helps him or her develop a stable and constructive value system. Some experts theorize that everyone is occasionally inclined toward delinquent behavior but that regard for these anchors restrains them.

Social anchors are especially hard for juveniles to find in areas undergoing rapid industrial and urban growth, and particularly where populations are transient. In these areas, society tends to become extremely disorganized. Eventually, businesses close and opportunities for employment disappear; neighborhoods and schools begin to decay; and wealthier families move out, leaving community and social institutions without support or influence. In the resulting disorder, many juveniles engage in delinquent behavior out of confusion and aimlessness, as well as the desire to obtain the material objects that people in more affluent neighborhoods have.

School

However, even when a child's environment is in upheaval, education can provide an extremely beneficial influence. Studies indicate that, when it comes to preventing delinquent behavior, a youngster's attachment to school can be even more important than his or her bond with parents. Children who do well in school win the approval of teachers and gain a measure of self-esteem. On the other hand, students with *learning disabilities* (disorders of the basic processes affecting how a child learns) often feel inadequate and overlooked. They may feel frustration and rage to the point that they behave aggressively and lash out against authority in an effort to draw attention to themselves.

Learning Disabilities

Classroom underachievement is the most common characteristic shared by juvenile delinquents. The symptoms of serious problems at

Students who do well in school, or learning-disabled students who get help, have shown low rates of juvenile delinquency. Yet classroom underachievement is a trait seen in many juvenile delinquents, whose feelings of frustration in school may lead them to resist various authority figures.

school are easily recognized: (1) low scores on achievement tests, (2) low grades, (3) a dislike of school, and (4) rejection of school authority. Juveniles with these problems often feel discouraged and alienated from their peers. Disapproval by their teachers and possibly their parents may cause these children to develop a bad attitude toward authority figures in general.

Avoiding these classroom problems may help the child escape delinquency. A 1976 study by the National Institute for Juvenile Justice and Delinquency Prevention estimated that 30% of juvenile delinquents are learning disabled. In addition, it showed a vast improvement among those delinquents who were placed in special programs designed to teach the learning disabled: Sixty percent of those in the special programs never broke the law again.

The fact that juvenile delinquents are typically underachievers does not necessarily mean they have below-average intelligence. Ford Foundation studies of major standardized tests of basic educational achievement indicate that the bottom one-fifth of the scores are concentrated in the population's minority and poorer members. For these students, many factors other than intelligence have influenced the results. Some of these young people have difficulty with English; others live in environments that do not value or encourage learning. Many of these families have never known anyone with a higher education and thus have never realized the benefits that education can bring.

A TRANSITORY PROBLEM?

Some theorists propose that some types of delinquent behavior are a normal part of every young person's maturation process, a behavior

Many young people experience a normal period of rebelliousness, as demonstrated by these mischievous boys. Most youngsters finally calm down: Only 10% of simple status offenders become criminals.

that most teenagers outgrow as they approach adulthood. A 1985 study by the Office of Juvenile Justice and Delinquency Prevention indicates that fewer than 10% of criminals begin their careers with status offenses. This suggests that ungovernable behavior, truancy, and underage alcohol consumption are transitory problems, largely stemming from youthful rebelliousness.

When it comes to delinquency offenses, however, statistics present a different story. According to 1987 juvenile court figures, the number of violations in every category of delinquency offense, including property, public order, person, and drug offenses, rises among older children. For example, the juvenile courts processed 51 out of every 1,000 delinquency cases involving 14 year olds. The rate for 15 year olds was 30% higher; for 16 year olds it was 59% higher; and for 17 year olds it was 72% higher.

The majority of referrals for all youth were for property offenses; however, rates for cases of drug-law violations showed the sharpest increase in the older age-groups. In fact, the rate of drug-law violation cases for 17 year olds was 377% greater than those for 14 year olds. The increasing rate of delinquency offenses according to age is particularly disturbing. It suggests that once a child starts on the path toward delinquency, the odds grow greater that he or she will continue there and eventually face the court system.

CHAPTER 5

THE YOUTH CULTURE

Many teenagers experiment with activities that imitate the behavior of irresponsible or hedonistic adults. The combination of some of these activities, such as drinking and driving, can be deadly.

Young people who exhibit antisocial behavior typically suffer from frustration caused by unfulfilled needs. One of young people's most crucial needs is the development of a sense of self-esteem. If parents' expectations for their child—to attain high grades, high social status, or athletic success—are too great, a youngster may not be able to build this confidence. Child abuse may also lead to a tragic absence of self-confidence. Moreover, as children mature, sexual frustrations among both heterosexual and homosexual teens become a source of insecurity. Any of these problems can lead young people to question their ability to control their environment or achieve their goals. These frustrations can afflict children anywhere, not simply those within a ghetto, ethnic group, or low economic level.

ADOLESCENCE

Adolescence is recognized as a tremendously difficult period in every person's life. Because many adolescents suffer from incessant emotional turmoil, impulsiveness and poor judgment lead many of them into delinquent behavior. Psychoanalyst Anna Freud described the troubling conflicts:

> It is normal for an adolescent to behave for a considerable length of time in an inconsistent and unpredictable manner, to fight impulses and to accept them; to ward them off successfully and to be overrun by them; to love his parents and to hate them; to revolt against them and to be dependent on them; to be deeply ashamed to acknowledge his mother before others, and unexpectedly to desire heart-to-heart talks with her; to thrive on imitation of and identification with others while searching unceasingly for his own identity; to be more idealistic, artistic, generous and unselfish than he will ever be again but also the opposite—self-centered, egotistic, calculating. Such fluctuations between extreme opposites would be deemed highly abnormal at any other time of life.

Adolescence also lasts longer in America than in many other countries as a result of trends in education. By the 1960s, a majority of all American high school students continued on to college, further postponing the assumption of adult responsibilities until age 21 or 22. With many young people going on to postgraduate studies, some parents support their children into their mid-twenties. As the renowned anthropologist Dr. Margaret Mead expressed it, the years of adolescence in America have "stretched out" considerably.

A SEPARATE CULTURE

With the separation of youth from the adult world and their isolation in the incubatorlike environment of high school, a youth culture developed that has been widely blamed for the incidence of juvenile delinquency, particularly that found among middle-class teenagers. In the collection of essays *A Theory of Middle-Class Juvenile Delinquency*, Ralph England points to several factors that have contributed to the development of the youth culture: (1) a marketplace that promotes the importance of material possessions and caters to young people who have money; (2) the rise of mass media communication influences; (3) the increase in publications that urge *hedonism*, a belief that pleasure is the primary goal in life; and (4) the emergence—and excess—of national concern over the emotional and behavioral problems of youth.

Cut off from the world of adults and deliberately distancing themselves from children, adolescents tend to create their own community with a distinct set of values, mode of dress, and style of speech. They use each other as reference points to establish status. Popularity becomes a major issue, making peer pressure an extremely powerful force in a teenager's life. Acceptance among peers is a natural response to the isolation imposed by adult expectations and restrictions.

Many theorists believe that the teenagers who are most involved in the youth culture are most likely to show delinquent behavior because their culture leans toward hedonistic and irresponsible behavior. Experts maintain that this behavior is not as serious as more violent offenses: It generally mimics that of hedonistic adults and tends to fall into the category of status, rather than delinquency, offenses. The experts believe that these status offenses surface as a facet of approved activities such as dating, sports, parties, and driving. Two examples are staying out late and engaging in sex. Yet other activities, such as joyriding and drinking, can be dangerous and even deadly.

Adult Influences

Juveniles basically learn their modes of behavior from the example of adults whom they respect. Unfortunately, fewer adults seem worthy of providing them with desirable role models. A study of American attitudes published in 1991 by the international advertising firm J. Walter Thompson may offer some of the reasons why juvenile delinquency is a growing problem in the United States. Published as a book entitled *The Day America Told the Truth—What People Really Believe About Everything That Matters*, it is an in-depth survey of what Americans really believe.

Authors James Patterson and Peter Kim claim that the survey reveals a country where individuals are making up their own moral codes. Responses indicate that only 13% of the population believe in all 10 biblical commandments and that 7% claim they would kill a stranger for $10 million. In addition, nearly one-third of all married Americans have had an affair. The authors conclude, "There is absolutely no moral consensus in this country—as there was in the 1950s and 1960s." If adults hope to control the problem of juvenile delinquency, they must try to raise their standards of thought and behavior to a level worthy of emulation by youth.

These juvenile textile workers in 1890 Philadelphia were strong enough to organize a strike. The child labor laws that followed such protests brought a change in children's roles, from overly responsible to highly protected.

A LACK OF STATUS

One theory attributes adolescent delinquency to the ill-defined social status of this age-group. In previous centuries, many young people made a major economic contribution to their families. They worked in the fields and the factories or learned trades as apprentices. Many colonial children earned their own living by the age of 10 or 12.

As laws were passed making education compulsory, however, children's productivity was reduced. In addition, labor laws raised the minimum age for employment to 16, so that young people were driven out of the factories and into the streets, where too much idle time led to mischief. At the same time that society limited the former functions of adolescents in ways that diminished their power, it failed to provide new functions to enhance their standing.

As a result of these changes, the American adolescent was confined to a kind of limbo, playing a minor and poorly conceived role some-where between childhood and adulthood. England describes the contradictions that modern adolescents face: They are unable to vote or hold public office yet are expected to be civic minded; excluded from challenging, full-time employment yet expected to spend their time constructively; discouraged from marrying early yet encouraged by advertising and liberal values to be sexually active.

MIDDLE-CLASS DELINQUENCY

The majority of America's teenagers live in middle-class families. Yet delinquency occurs even in these homes where young people appear to have every advantage and every reason to be model children: Their families are intact, they are well provided for, and they may be preparing for college and careers. Yet their behavior is antisocial.

Through his lifelong work with juvenile delinquents in Kentucky, Falcon Baker observed that the psychological abuse that can produce juvenile delinquency is particularly common among upwardly mobile, middle-class families. Parents may continually hound children to succeed in ways that feel unlikely or unnatural to the child because he or she lacks the necessary interest or ability. Overprotective parents may

Actor James Dean played the lead character in the 1955 film Rebel Without a Cause. *The story deals with three middle-class teenagers whose delinquent actions result from unhappy family situations.*

also place the most unreasonable restrictions on their children at the precise moment when the child is feeling adventurous or trying to assert his or her independence.

Confused Parental Roles

Some theorists attribute middle-class delinquency to parental confusion over child rearing. Certain middle-class parents—typically well educated, materialistic, and ambitious—have tried to follow the advice of modern-day experts on raising children. As a result, they have studied and tried to implement methods that are often contradictory, experimental, and overly permissive. This inconsistent style of parenting can produce disoriented, unmanageable, and spoiled young people.

For example, some parents try to be friends and confidants to their children rather than authoritative disciplinarians. They later discover that this particular role requires more time and energy than they have to give. Parents who feel guilty about their inability to give their children enough attention may shower them with gifts and entertainment instead. As a result, some youths associate material things and pleasures with affection and acceptance. This also encourages the hedonistic tendencies that may lead to delinquent behavior.

The Effort to Get Ahead

The recent increase in households in which both parents pursue careers may also contribute to the problem of middle-class juvenile delinquency. *Latchkey* children, who come home from school to an empty house, typically are unsupervised until late in the day when their parents arrive. Expected to be more responsible because both parents spend so much time out of the house, these children are sometimes inclined to abuse the freedom that comes with responsibility. One reason for this could be immaturity; another could be the need for attention.

Another disturbing factor in young peoples' lives is the middle-class family's willingness to move in order to get ahead. Many parents raise children in towns where they have no relatives. They have no grandparents nearby to serve as backup authority figures, to transmit stabilizing values, and to help with child-rearing responsibilities. Often no aunts, uncles, or cousins are available to reinforce a child's sense of identity and belonging. On the other hand, children who live near relatives—individuals who have a vested interest in the child's up-bringing and a natural sense of responsibility for his or her well-being—are more likely to mature without showing delinquent behavior.

Different Offenses

Empey observes that individuals in the middle-class youth culture tolerate destructive acts such as letting the air out of tires, fighting,

Crack Kids

Despite efforts to educate young people about birth control, teenage pregnancy is not decreasing: In 1990 approximately 1 out of every 20 females under the age of 20 gave birth. A pregnant teenager faces many problems, and these difficulties can only increase if the mother uses drugs. A pregnant woman on crack, for example, greatly increases her risk of having a child with birth defects.

The National Association for Perinatal Addiction Research and Education estimates that 375,000 out of approximately 4 million babies born each year have been exposed to illegal drugs in the womb. Most of them are *crack babies* who are born to mothers who abuse crack. They are easily identified by their undersized bodies and small heads, the latter being a trait often associated with low IQ. Many are particularly lethargic and have chronic seizures. As they get older, they may have difficulty learning to talk and have impaired motor and social skills. Unfortunately, most of these babies are born in ghettos, where even healthy children are disadvantaged by poverty, neglect, and violence.

Often, these infants cannot tell the difference between their mother and strangers and do not respond to their caretakers with affection. They may be moody, easily distracted, and prone to erupt in violent and self-destructive frenzies. Concerned citizens are beginning to fear that the crack children will grow into a new generation of juvenile delinquents who are more dangerous and destructive than any seen before.

The first large group of crack children was born in the mid-1980s, so physicians, social workers, and educators are just beginning to understand the enormity of the problem and devise ways to help. A 1991 article in *Time* magazine points out that the cost of hospital care for crack babies is about 13 times as expensive as that for a healthy newborn

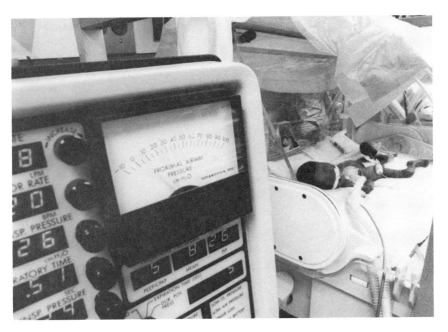

Compared with healthy newborns, crack babies require a tremendous amount of care. As they grow, they also need the type of education geared toward mentally and emotionally challenged children.

($6,900 compared with $522). The article also reports that in Boston the cost of one year of special education for such a child is more than twice as expensive as a regular public school education ($13,000 compared with $5,000). The government must meet other expenses as well, such as the cost of placing these children in foster homes in an effort to compensate for their numerous disadvantages.

Some enraged citizens believe that the courts should prosecute mothers whose drug abuse has harmed their babies. They say that using crack is a crime and claim that the newborn's appearance presents obvious evidence that the baby was exposed to illegal drugs in the womb. Most experts, however, prefer to concentrate their efforts on helping the children. But the full extent of the crack babies' handicaps or how much time, energy, and money it will take to overcome these difficulties remains to be seen.

A nationwide survey of high school seniors estimates that in 1989 more than twice as many white males as black males used cocaine. White male high school seniors also reported higher rates of marijuana use.

breaking street lights, ripping antennae off cars, and vandalizing schools. However, they draw the line at assault, armed robbery, and burglary. In fact, William Kvaraceus and Walter B. Miller, in their essay *Norm-Violating Behavior in Middle-Class Culture*, suggest that when a middle-class adolescent commits a serious delinquency offense, he or she is probably displaying *pathological* (mentally abnormal) rather than group-supported behavior. These young people are often sent to private institutions where they receive psychiatric treatment.

THE DRUG CULTURE

Since 1975, the University of Michigan Institute for Social Research has conducted an annual nationwide survey of 70,000 high school seniors. The survey shows that the use of illicit drugs, specifically marijuana, peaked in 1979 and has decreased every year since. Cocaine use peaked in 1986, coinciding with the highly publicized cocaine-related death of two sports idols, University of Maryland basketball star Len Bias and Cleveland Browns defensive back Don Rogers. Bias's death was especially dramatic because he had been the first pick of the Boston Celtics in the 1986 draft.

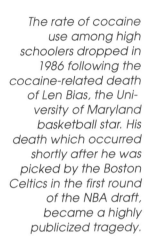

The rate of cocaine use among high schoolers dropped in 1986 following the cocaine-related death of Len Bias, the University of Maryland basketball star. His death which occurred shortly after he was picked by the Boston Celtics in the first round of the NBA draft, became a highly publicized tragedy.

Although society in general seems to have decreased its drug usage, today's American public is concerned that drug abuse is spreading like a cancer in the ghettos. Some statistics support the view that the drug problem is escalating among the nation's poor and minority populations. Juvenile court statistics for 1987 show that the rate in juvenile drug-law violations was 106% greater among nonwhites than among whites. They also indicate that between 1986 and 1987, juvenile drug-offense cases increased 27.5% among nonwhites while decreasing 7.6% among whites.

However, a more recent University of Michigan survey shows unexpected results for the years 1985 through 1989. It found that nearly twice as many white male high school seniors (11.9%) as black male high school seniors (6.1%) reported having used cocaine within the past year. Among females, 4.1% of white seniors had used cocaine within the previous year, compared with 1.3% of black seniors. Marijuana usage rates among white males was 40%, compared with 29.8% among black males; among white females it was 36%, compared with 18.4% among black females. Nearly half of the white males admitted to having had 5 drinks at one time in the previous 2 weeks, compared with 24% of black males.

Yet the University of Michigan survey does not include statistics on some important factors. For example, the survey does not account for drug use among young people who have already dropped out of school. It also does not investigate the use of *crack*, a form of cocaine that produces an instant and intense euphoria and then leaves the addict desperate for another hit in about 20 minutes. This desperation leads to intense feelings of frustration and irritability that may result in violent outbursts. Many young people are unwilling to admit using crack, so it is a difficult problem to measure.

Even though middle-class juveniles have more advantages than their peers in the ghettos, both groups of young people share the same basic needs. They are searching for self-esteem, a sense of belonging, and a personal attachment to individuals that offer stabilizing influences. Unfortunately, when young people find no help for meeting these needs, they may turn to drugs in an effort to escape feelings of despair, emptiness, and fear.

CHAPTER 6

THE AMERICAN YOUTH GANG

Southern Los Angeles is America's largest stronghold for modern gangs. This photo was taken during a series of late 1980s police raids intended to weaken the ever-growing power of the city's gangs.

No aspect of juvenile delinquency strikes more fear into the hearts of Americans than gang violence. Unpredictable, unexplained, and often performed with sophisticated weapons by youths who may be too drugged to feel fear or pain, gang violence is becoming increasingly common.

A study of 900 cities done by Walter B. Miller for the federal government in 1975 identified about 105,000 gangs in the United States. They included more than 1.6 million members, typically between the ages of 8 and 25. A *U.S. News and World Report* article in April 1991 indicates that gangs have doubled their size in recent years. Within the Los Angeles area, they have grown from approximately 400 gangs with 45,000 members in 1985 to 800 gangs with 90,000 members in 1990.

Gangs thrive in the ghettos among impoverished ethnic groups, announcing their presence with graffiti and distinctive colors, clothes, gestures, walks, and jargon. Gangs meet a universal need among young people—the desire to feel important, to find excitement, and to enjoy the material things in life. Often they offer protection and acceptance to ghetto youths who come from broken homes with little security.

Gangs meet the fundamental yearning to belong. In 1990, *Harper's* magazine illustrated that point in an interview with members of the famous Los Angeles gangs, the Bloods and the Crips. (These 2 groups originated in southern California about 20 years ago and now have affiliates in 32 states and 113 cities.) One former member named Tee explained, "What I think is formulating here is that human nature wants to be accepted. A human being gives less of a damn what he is accepted into. At that age—11 to 17—all kids want to belong. They are un-people."

Gangs are supremely powerful in a territory they have staked out as their own—a territory that may encompass city blocks or cover a street corner. They have a recognized leader, who is usually supported by a group of lieutenants. Often gangs have an apartment or an abandoned building where members meet and sleep. Each gang has rules and traditions to reinforce its unity, and all gangs demand absolute loyalty.

YESTERDAY AND TODAY

Gangs have made their mark in congested American cities since the early 19th century, when large groups of immigrants first felt the crush of poverty and prejudice. The first gang to appear, the Forty Thieves in New York City, was composed mainly of adult men. It was organized in 1826 by a man named Edward Coleman who was later hanged in Tombs Prison for murdering his wife.

According to James Haskins, author of *Street Gangs Yesterday and Today*, the Forty Thieves congregated at a greengrocer's between robbings, beatings, and killings of well-dressed people who ventured into their territory. They were soon followed by the Kerryonians, a group who came from County Kerry in Ireland. In fact, most of America's early gangs were formed by the Irish, who at that time were the poorest of the nation's immigrants and subject to harsh discrimination.

Status

Early gang members were often outsiders who banded together to find support, and they devised unusual names to establish their group's identity. The Roach Guards hung out in a liquor store owned by a man named Roach. The Plug Uglies were exceptionally large and wore plug hats stuffed with wool and leather for protection during battle. The Shirt Tales always wore their shirts untucked. The Dead Rabbits went into battle carrying a dead rabbit impaled on a stake; the term *dead rabbit* used to refer to a tough guy. Other names, which made the members' need for status painfully obvious, included the Ambassadors, the Dukes, the Imperial Counts, and the Viceroys.

Early gangs also wore distinctive and colorful clothes. Each gang's colors were often displayed in the stripes on their pants. Similarly, today's gang members may show their colors on a jacket, a T-shirt, a bandanna worn on the head, or a stripe on their running shoes. Other gangs may show no obvious sign at all. In *Harper's* magazine, Tee explains that gang members can identify each other without obvious colors or symbols. "Police officers can recognize police officers, athletes can recognize athletes, gay people can recognize gay people. Well, we can recognize each other. It's simple."

One way that gang members can identify each other without a visible sign is through language. Tee comments on the special speech patterns developed by gangs: "If it's a Blood set [gang], they use a *k* [or a *b*] instead of a *c* . . . See, Bloods don't say *c*'s and Crips don't say *b*'s. To a Blood, a cigarette is a *bigarette*. And Crips don't say *because*, they say *cecause*."

Gangs enjoy the attention of the media. These members of a 1940s gang called the Zoot Suiters publicly offered to make a truce between rival gangs in Los Angeles.

Publicity

Despite these codes, gang members are not too concerned about hiding their identity. From the beginning, America's gangs have been interested in publicity. Following the Civil War, one of the first people to document gangs was a Danish photojournalist named Jacob A. Riis. He found members eager to be interviewed and photographed. Gangs found that attention from the press also brought them more power.

The tradition of seeking publicity has grown today to the point that gangs may erupt in violence in attempts to gain media attention. Early in 1991, 4 members of the Orientals took 40 hostages in a Sacramento, California, appliance store with an announcement that they were seeking publicity for their gang. They paid a high price for the attention they received: Three hostages and three of the four gang members were killed.

THE MODERN ERA

The era of the modern youth gang began after World War II, when crime and violence rose sharply. This increase was traced to young people between the ages of 13 and 20, who suddenly became more rebellious, defiant, and destructive than they had ever been before. The reason for this has never been satisfactorily explained, but in their book *Youth Gangs*, Edward F. Dolan, Jr., and Shan Finney comment that "it seemed as if the horrors of the war had left behind a sense of unrest and even frenzy that was affecting many people."

As a huge influx of blacks and Puerto Ricans moved into the northern cities, the new gangs became primarily younger and nonwhite. According to Haskins, more of them also carried firearms, and their activities began to center around large-scale and deadly street fighting. These new gangs had a more rigid structure with titled leadership, grouping by age, and federations with other gangs. Additionally, the use of drugs became more publicized.

DRUGS AND GANGS

Drugs have always been a part of gang life. Herbert Asbury, who wrote a history of New York gangs in 1927, estimated that 90% of one group called the Hudson Dusters were cocaine addicts. He reported, "When under the influence of the drug [they] were very dangerous, for they were insensible to ordinary punishment, and were possessed of great, if artificial, bravery and ferocity."

Because gangs are well positioned to profit within ghettos, they are often involved in the spread of drug use in these poverty-stricken areas. Older members frequently pay younger ones to deliver drugs, knowing that juveniles get lighter sentences.

Publicity concerning the negative effects of drugs has helped reduce recreational substance abuse. But when drugs are used as an escape from everyday life, the problem is more difficult to control or to change. This occurs primarily in the nation's ghettos where, as Falcon Baker comments, "For a little while rage and hostility are rocked to sleep by the narcotic effect. There is peace in the soul no longer tormented by the sense of perpetual failure, by the feelings of inferiority, by the pains of discrimination."

Because they are located in ghettos, gangs are in a prime position to supply this need for drugs. They are also relatively well organized and equipped. Additionally, older gang members have a somewhat sophisticated knowledge of the law. As a result, they make juveniles a mainstay of their cocaine supply-and-distribution systems in order to escape tough sentences for themselves if they are involved in a drug bust. As Falcon Baker observes, it is not unusual for 11 or 12 year olds to earn $100 a day as lookouts or $300 a day as *runners* (messengers who deliver drugs).

Although only about 6% of delinquency offenses are drug viola-tions, that figure misrepresents the extent of the problem among juveniles. There is no way to measure how many drug violations are linked to gangs, but they are deeply involved in the drug culture. They are part of the spreading problem of crack addiction. Many acts of violence are committed under the influence of drugs, and many thefts are committed for money to buy drugs. The former director of the National Drug Control Policy, William Bennett (often called the "drug czar"), pointed out that a thief gets only 10% of the value of anything he or she fences, so he or she must steal $600 worth of goods each day to support a $60-a-day drug habit. That amounts to $219,000 a year.

GANG HIERARCHY AND ORGANIZATION

Approximately 90% of American gang members are male, most of them between the ages of 13 and 24. Among these young people, Dolan and Finney explain, there are different degrees of gang involvement, including leaders and *associate* and *fringe* members. Gang leaders have risen through the ranks for qualities that gang members admire most—

Each gang establishes different goals. In a plot to take over New York City, this group of 7 young people committed 15 holdups. The 1965 gang was equipped with a machine gun and 100 rounds of ammunition.

bravado, cleverness, toughness, and the ability to make money from drugs, theft, and sometimes the *protection racket* (promising to keep dangerous gang members at bay for a fee).

As a result of these qualities, such members acquire a following, which typically emerges from the hard-core members who identify closely with the gang and are determined to keep it going. Leaders retain their position, however, only by continually thinking of things to do that interest or benefit their members. The position is by no means stable. The tide of loyalty can shift instantly to another member if the leader makes a mistake, shows any weakness, or is outdone by somebody else with a more daring or lucrative idea.

Associates run with the gang all the time and wear the jacket, T-shirt, colors, or other necessary symbol of membership. They are not, however, at the center of the gang's life and activities. They are not responsible for thinking up things for members to do or for organizing parties or crime sprees. Fringe members are even less involved, dropping in and out of the gang for a variety of reasons. They may participate in gang activities because they have some valuable skill or knowledge, want to help revenge a friend who is a gang member, or are liked or respected for some personal quality. They may turn out for a fight, any sort of mischief, or a power struggle of some kind, but they do not identify completely with the gang.

STRESS AMONG MEMBERS

Becoming a member of a particular gang often means paying a high price. Haskins describes the amount of stress involved in being a gang member: "You *had* to be tough, you *had* to revenge every slight, you *had* to carry a piece or a knife, and you *had* to use it or someone else would use theirs on you. You had to be on guard all the time, you could never relax."

Machismo

In *Youth Gangs*, Dolan and Finney explain that Hispanic gang members in particular stress the concept of *machismo*, a view of manhood that requires a male to fight any threat against his masculinity. Gang members must always be on guard against efforts to intimidate or dominate them or to attack their courage and honor. The issue of their manhood is never settled; they have to fight again and again, caught in a vicious cycle that leads to escalating violence. An Arizona gang member quoted in *Youth Gangs* illustrates the dilemma:

> This guy, Manuel, he comes at me, see, and so I send him the hospital. Well, now he's the one that's on the spot. He's not the macho guy everybody thought he was. So he has to get back at me, and he's got to work me over worse than I did him. Maybe he wins. Now it's my turn. I gotta go at him. Man, it can go on forever, getting worse all the time.

Loyalty

Some gang members believe the greatest glory would be to die for their gang. Members who try to switch to another gang may have to kill a member of their former gang to prove their loyalty. The gang they have abandoned may hunt them indefinitely. For some gang members, the only escape from all the tension and fear is through drugs—drugs they cannot afford unless they commit crimes. This creates another cycle of entrapment.

TYPES OF GANGS

According to Dolan and Finney, destructive gang activities fall into three general categories: (1) criminal, (2) violent, and (3) turf control.

The 1961 film West Side Story *is a modern-day retelling of the classic* Romeo and Juliet. *The star-crossed lovers are associated with rival gangs, whose feud is based on ethnic differences.*

Criminal gangs are interested in making money, often by trying to control illegal drug traffic or prostitution in a city or neighborhood. Violent gangs, whose members may be emotionally unstable, are bent on destroying property and hurting people, often at random. Turf control gangs want to be in charge of everything that goes on in a particular territory, especially among the young people there.

A gang's preference for specific sorts of crimes may also depend on its ethnic group. Dolan and Finney estimate that almost 90% of gang members are minority members—47% are black, 35% are Hispanic, and 7.5% are Asian. The remaining 10% of gang members are white. Each ethnic group expresses distinctive traits, such as the clothes they wear and the lingo they use. These differences are often attributed to values that immigrants carried over from more traditional cultures. For example, Hispanic gangs are extremely aware of turf control because Hispanic culture has traditionally stressed the value of land.

Despite the obvious danger and ignorance of many gang activities, these groups continue to attract antisocial juveniles—particularly those living in ghettos. Leaders armed with weapons such as Uzis, as well as the traditional handguns, brass knuckles, *blackjacks* (a hand weapon made of metal enclosed in leather), bicycle chains, clubs, and ice picks, make ghetto youths see the gang's menace as an "escape from power-lessness," according to Haskins. Their ability to use force offers an escape from feeling like a nobody, a condition that often results from poverty and illiteracy.

CHAPTER 7

CHANGES AHEAD

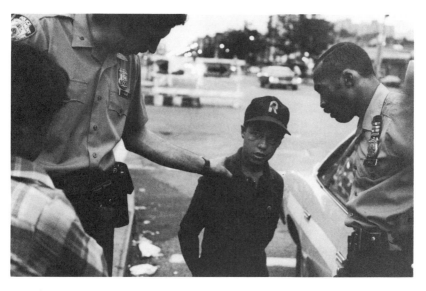

New York City police must stop two boys from fighting in the street. Is this normal youthful behavior or a tendency that should be prevented early in life?

In the past 400 years, the Western world's attitude toward children has changed from one of indifference to one of intense concern. America seems to have taken this trend to the extreme. In her 1970 book, *The Culture of Childhood*, Mary E. Goodman commented, "We have set a new record; no other people seem ever to have been so preoccupied with children." The question now is whether that trend has reached its peak and what will happen next.

THE EFFECT OF THE BABY BOOM

In the second half of the 20th century, much of the American interest in children has been driven by the sheer number of them. Immediately after World War II, when returning servicemen started having families, a remarkable surge in births occurred in the United States as well as in many other parts of the world. In most countries, the surge lasted from three to six years. In the United States, however, it continued for almost 20 years.

Of approximately 240 million Americans in the present population, about one-third were born between the years 1946 and 1964. Referred to as the *baby boomers*, this group is so large that *demographers*, specialists in population statistics, have compared it to "a pig moving through a python." The large number of baby boomers has enabled their age-group to dominate the needs, desires, and interests of American markets, politics, and entertainment since the late 1940s.

Dr. Ken Dychtwald, author of *Age Wave* and an expert on aging patterns in America, follows the tracks left by the first baby boomers. The early years, he notes, brought skyrocketing sales of diapers, baby food, and toys. As the group entered school, construction of educational facilities boomed. The rage for television shows such as "The Mickey Mouse Club," "Captain Kangaroo," and "Ozzie and Harriet" corresponded to the rising number of young television viewers. A few years after that, burgeoning sales of soft drinks, movie tickets, records, and fast foods accompanied baby boomers through their teenage years.

As the younger of the baby boomers grew older, many of the markets they had dominated for 20 years began to shrink. As these young people reached their late teens, however, they popularized marijuana smoking—raising the profits of a cigarette-paper manufacturer by 25% for a decade. When the baby boomers became politically rebellious, the country was convulsed by demonstrations. When they became introspective in their twenties, self-help books sold like hotcakes. When they moved deep into their careers in the 1980s, business publications thrived.

All the baby boomers have now grown up; the oldest are approaching 50 and the youngest, 30. This is causing the nation as a whole to mature. Dychtwald points out that in July 1983, the number of Americans over the age of 65 surpassed the number of teenagers for the first time. "The era of the United States as a youth-focused nation is coming to an end," he asserts, "and it will not be seen again in our lifetimes."

This trend in aging is a natural progression, but it will have an unprecedented effect in America as the bulge of baby boomers moves into old age. As they head toward retirement, the baby boomers are becoming preoccupied with issues of security—the desire to protect their families, their homes, their possessions, and themselves from harm. Their politics typically become more conservative, and they are more interested in the issues of their own generation, such as raising taxes to protect the Social Security Trust Fund rather than to improve secondary education.

In addition, the aging baby boomers may not be especially concerned about juvenile needs because (for many of them) their interests have never focused on children. Estimates claim that 20% of baby boomers will have no children at all and 25% will have only one. Some people fear that this lack of involvement with young people will

On their way to a sand-lot football game, these Philadelphia youngsters stopped to search for drugs in abandoned crack vials. People are highly concerned about violent outbursts caused by this extremely addictive form of cocaine.

undermine traditional support of educational and tax-funded programs for children. Whether this distance from youth will affect national policy remains to be seen.

Despite a declining interest in children, it appears that the number of young people between the ages of 5 and 17 will rise by the year 2000. Although the number of youths in this age-group dropped 3.4% from 1980 to 1990, the Census Bureau projects that this age-group will increase by 7% in the next decade. According to Charles Patrick Ewing in *Kids Who Kill*, if the number of juveniles increases by 7%, then the rate of juvenile crime will increase at a similar, or greater, rate—unless the justice system or society somehow reverses the present trend toward crime.

CHILDREN AND THEIR RIGHTS REEXAMINED

Early Americans did not generally believe that the Bill of Rights applied to children. In addition they believed that the state was empowered to act as a child's guardian when necessary, even if this meant taking away his or her liberty in a tyrannical and arbitrary fashion. Nonetheless, on the issue of rights, American children have gained ground rapidly in the 20th century. In fact, some critics argue that children now have more rights than they have the maturity to exercise responsibly.

Children's rights activists have progressed on additional issues since the 1960s Supreme Court decisions ensuring children the same constitutional protection that adults enjoy. In 1971, the voting age was lowered to 18 when the nation yielded to the popular argument: If 18 year olds are old enough to be drafted and possibly die for their country, they are old enough to vote.

Some states have lowered the age at which children can leave school to 16. Certain states have also passed legislation allowing minors to consent to their own medical treatment for sexually transmitted diseases, drug and alcohol dependency, and contraception. In some states, teenagers also have the right to have an abortion without parental consent.

Emancipation

In certain states, juveniles can appeal to a legal process called *emancipation*, which was designed to officially free children from the custody, care, and control of their parents before the age of 18. One well-known case involved the young entertainer Tiffany, who wished to gain control of the money she made. In addition, most states automatically consider minors emancipated who are married or enlisted in the armed services.

Before a minor can be emancipated, the court must decide whether this legal action is in the child's best interest. The minor must also prove that he or she is self-supporting. Some states additionally require that the minor live apart from his or her parents and also that the parents give their consent to emancipation. Even after emancipation, some states still do not permit the juvenile to consume alcohol until the age of 21.

Kojak, a 13-year-old drug dealer, returns from a shopping trip with friends. Juvenile offenders, who are getting involved with serious crime at increasingly younger ages, often do not fear getting caught because they expect lenient sentences.

A Former Offender's Outlook

Andrés V., now 27, was first sentenced as a juvenile offender at age 16. He is now a counselor at the Fortune Society in New York City. This program helps juveniles and adults who are on parole or have been released from prison find jobs, become better educated, and face the feelings involved in readjusting to everyday life.

Andrés describes his own experiences in the juvenile and adult justice systems and the impact they had on his life:

"I started using drugs at age 12 or 13 and was thrown out of school in Brooklyn. At age 16, I was arrested for armed robbery. I got six years and was sent to a section [of a juvenile facility] for adolescents. I was crazy there. Most of the guys knew about my reputation on the street because I knew a lot of people in the Bronx and Brooklyn who I met again in prison. I learned more about the street from some guys I met there. They were homeboys, friends from your crew who run the prison. They came up with better ideas about how to get more money. That's what prison does. Instead of rehabilitating you, it educates you about the street.

"The parole board let me out in six months, but when I got back to the street I was worse. I got a job, but I quit right away. I kept seeing my parole officer, so he didn't know. I could make more money on the street, and by robbing people. I had two months and six days on the street until I got arrested again, but this time it was worse—for armed robbery and kidnapping.

"I pleaded guilty and expected to get 9 to 10 years, but in a trial I probably would have got 12 to 25 years. I was 17 and got a 7-to-14 year sentence plus 3 years I owed for breaking parole. When I first went in again, I'd do things to impress people. I got my role models from other criminals and drug dealers, living what they call the fast life—money, cars, women.

"My first few years in prison I was doing things to fit in. I was young, but people looked up to me. I liked to fight, so I spent some time in my first years in the box. Solitary confinement is one of the worst things. One time I spent 120 days in the box; I had one hour outside every day when I saw other people. The police serve you food and you don't get enough.

"I had been through a lot of prisons. I started a riot, so I got thrown out of one. I was in a medium security prison, but then I went to maximum security. There the police are strict; you know they're tough. I swung at a police officer one time and they beat me up, broke my head and my teeth. That taught me a lesson [that brought a change in attitude].

"Then I had to prove I could be trusted. Greenhaven [an adult facility in New York State] was a prison that taught me a lot. I learned to type and use the computer. I helped implement a program to help inmates prepare to go home. I became a director of prerelease and an intermediary with the administration. I worked with Latinos in Progress and translated for Hispanic prisoners.

"Prisons have schools, but they're not mandatory. You work 2 hours a day for 30 cents an hour. If the prisons taught a trade and paid minimum wage, they could have the prisoners pay for their room and their clothes while incarcerated. The inmates would learn to get up and go to work. When an inmate goes back to society he would have a skill. Now when he goes to the street, he does what he knows how to do—85% to 90% of those released within 6 months come back to prison. Prison is not a place for nobody. If I get arrested again, I'll be in for 25 years. I don't want to be in for the rest of my life."

Childhood—Gone for Good?

Those adults who oppose the children's rights movement say that they want to ensure that children have time to enjoy a safe and carefree childhood. They hope to provide young people with the opportunity to experience the ideal childhood—an extended period of time to grow up in a leisurely fashion, free of adult worries and responsibilities until they have gained the necessary preparation. Unfortunately, this ideal seems increasingly unrealistic in an era faced with unrelenting social problems.

Even when children are able to enjoy an innocent and untroubled time, it often seems far too brief. As early as elementary school, American children are dealing with issues such as suicide, drug addiction, child abuse, AIDS, and gun sales. Often they lack the maturity to understand the consequences of their actions—a problem that may add to the growing rate of serious juvenile offenses. As children rush

Kojak cries when released from a Philadelphia jail. His sister, an occasional drug user, comforts him. Juvenile advocacy groups constantly search for new ways to help young people without resorting to penal institutions.

toward adolescence with awesome worldliness, more people are questioning the basic concept of the juvenile court system—that childhood is an innocent time requiring special treatment. People are becoming increasingly critical of the juvenile court's commitment to rehabilitation and its reluctance to punish juveniles for serious wrongdoing.

ANOTHER LOOK AT PUNISHMENT

Thus far the juvenile courts have shown no sign of success at rehabilitating delinquents. If the juvenile courts fail to rehabilitate the juvenile, and the criminal courts fail to punish the adult, then how effective can they be in preventing crime?

In recent years, people have become increasingly aware of flaws in the justice system. Convicted criminals are serving only a small part of their sentence before being freed. In 1991, for example, the Texas Board of Pardons and Parole estimated that the average inmate serves only three weeks of every year for which he or she is sentenced—less than one-seventeenth of the sentence handed down by the courts. State district judge Ted Poe comments, "Defendants are finding that they are spending so little time in prison for a crime that crime does in fact pay." Of course, juvenile delinquents are as aware of this situation as adult criminals and are becoming less concerned about getting caught.

In frustration, people are examining the issue of punishment. Because modern juveniles seem increasingly capable of violent crimes at earlier ages, society is beginning to take a different stance toward the court's previous tradition of leniency. Baker points out that criminologists have long known that "the key to deterring a person [young or old] from crime is the certainty of punishment, not the severity of the punishment." For this reason, some people propose shifting crime control back to a more dependable form of punishment. They suggest establishing stricter standards for probation and parole, requiring offenders to serve the entire amount of time for which they are sentenced. Some opponents suggest abolishing the juvenile court system in favor of treating and trying young offenders as adults.

Although many youngsters come from tragic family circumstances, community-based programs may help them overcome these disadvantages. In New York City, Mother Hale has developed a program to care for the troubled children of drug-addicted mothers.

EFFORTS AT PREVENTION

Other people focus on continuing with present methods of crime prevention. They concentrate on providing opportunities that give juveniles a greater stake in conformity. Some programs offer responsible child care for youths suffering from neglect, abuse, exploitation, and other aspects of poverty and discrimination. Others create jobs to give adolescents the training and experience to earn decent incomes.

Efforts to prevent teen pregnancy through education and to provide teen mothers with the support they need to become good parents, complete their educations, and train for a job if necessary, are under way. Schools are directing more resources toward children with learning and language disabilities who are growing up in homes where parents or guardians are illiterate or do not value education.

Recent reform efforts have shown that higher success rates occur in smaller programs based within communities. For example, housing juvenile offenders in homier, community-based residences with fewer roommates allows young people to develop a more positive outlook than they would in a large, impersonal institution. In a smaller residence, they get personal attention from educators, psychologists, and social workers, enabling them to adjust to society in a more humane environment.

One newly attempted community program is Teens on Target, an educational program established in Oakland, California, that encourages teenagers to resolve problems with violence in healthy ways. Student volunteers—many of whom had previously relied on violent ways of expressing themselves—are taught violence-prevention methods for dealing with guns, drugs, and abusive family and social situations. These young people are then sent to teach these techniques to kids in their own age-group in public schools.

In addition to these ongoing efforts, other reformers stress the importance of helping younger children. People are realizing that efforts to prevent delinquency must begin as early in a child's life as possible. Baker comments, "Showing concern for these troubled juveniles in their teens is at least a decade too late." Although the rate of juvenile crime may worsen before it improves, perhaps its severity will lead adults to reexamine their views and influences on children.

APPENDIX:
FOR MORE INFORMATION

The following is a list of organizations that can provide further information about juvenile delinquency and related topics.

GENERAL INFORMATION

American Justice Institute
705 Merchant Street
Sacramento, CA 95814
(916) 442-0707

National Center for Juvenile Justice
701 Forbes Avenue
Pittsburgh, PA 15219
(412) 227-6950

National Council on Crime and
    Delinquency
685 Market Street, Suite 620
San Francisco, CA 94105
(415) 896-6223

National Crime Prevention Council
1700 K Street, NW
Second Floor
Washington, DC 20006
(202) 466-6272

National Institute of Justice
National Criminal Justice Reference
    Service
Department F
Box 6000

Rockville, MD 20850
(800) 851-3420
(301) 251-5500
(from metropolitan Washington, DC,
    and Maryland)

U.S. Department of Justice
Office of Juvenile Justice and
    Delinquency Prevention
633 Indiana Avenue, NW, Room 1100
Washington, DC 20531
(202) 307-0751

University of Illinois at Chicago
Department of Psychiatry
Institute for Juvenile Research
907 South Walcott Avenue
Chicago, IL 60612
(312) 413-1772

AGENCIES FOR FORMER OFFENDERS

The Door
121 Sixth Avenue
New York, NY 10013
(212) 941-9090

Fortune Society
39 West 19th Street
New York, NY 10011
(212) 206-0707

CHILD ABUSE

American Humane Association
63 Inverness Drive, East
Englewood, CO 80112
(303) 792-5333

Clearinghouse on Child Abuse and
    Neglect Information
P.O. Box 1182
Washington, DC 20013
(703) 821-2086

Giarretto Institute
P.O. Box 952
San Jose, CA 95108
(408) 453-7616

National Council on Child Abuse and
    Family Violence
1155 Connecticut Avenue, NW, Suite
    400
Washington, DC 20036
(202) 429-6695

National Exchange Club Foundation for
    the Prevention of Child Abuse
3050 Central Avenue
Toledo, OH 43606
(419) 535-3232

DRUG ABUSE

American Council for Drug Education
204 Monroe Street, Suite 100
Rockville, MD 20850
(301) 294-0600

Council on Drug Abuse
698 Weston Road, Suite 17
Toronto, Ontario M6N 3R3
Canada
(416) 763-1491

Straight, Inc.
3001 Grandy Blvd.
St. Petersburg, FL 33702
(813) 576-8929

Target—Helping Students Cope with
    Alcohol and Drugs
P.O. Box 20626
11724 Plaza Circle
Kansas City, MO 64195
(816) 464-5400

FURTHER READING

Ariès, Philippe. *Centuries of Childhood: A Social History of Family Life.* New York: Random House, 1965.

Baker, Falcon. *Saving Our Kids from Delinquency, Drugs, and Despair.* New York: HarperCollins, 1991.

Bloch, Herbert A., and Arthur Niederhoffer. *The Gang: A Study in Adolescent Behavior.* Westport, CT: Greenwood Press, 1976.

Bortner, M. A. *Delinquency and Justice: An Age of Crisis.* New York: McGraw-Hill, 1988.

Carpenter, Cheryl, et al. *Kids, Drugs, and Crime.* Lexington, MA: Lexington Books, 1987.

Cohen, A. K. *Delinquent Boys: The Culture of the Gang.* New York: Free Press, 1955.

Davis, James R. *Street Gangs: Youth, Biker, and Prison Groups.* Dubuque, IA: Kendall/Hunt, 1982.

Dolan, Edward F., Jr., and Shan Finney. *Youth Gangs.* Englewood Cliffs, NJ: Messner, 1984.

Dychtwald, Ken, and Joe Flower. *Age Wave.* Los Angeles: Tarcher, 1989.

Empey, LaMar T. *American Delinquency: Its Meaning and Construction.* Chicago: Dorsey Press, 1978.

Ewing, Charles Patrick. *Kids Who Kill.* Lexington, MA: Lexington Books, 1990.

Fabricant, Michael. *Juveniles in the Family Courts.* Lexington, MA: Lexington Books, 1982.

Fox, Sanford J. *The Law of Juvenile Courts in a Nutshell.* St. Paul, MN: West, 1984.

Gilbert, James B. *A Cycle of Outrage: America's Reaction to the Juvenile Delinquent in the 1950's.* New York: Oxford University Press, 1986.

Glueck, Sheldon S., and Eleanor T. Glueck. *Juvenile Delinquents Grown Up.* Millwood, NY: Kraus Reprint and Periodicals, 1940.

Greenleave, Barbara Kaye. *Children Through the Ages.* New York: McGraw-Hill, 1978.

Haskins, James. *Street Gangs: Yesterday and Today.* New York: Hastings House, 1977.

Hawes, Joseph M. *Children in Urban Society: Juvenile Delinquency in Nineteenth-Century America.* New York: Oxford University Press, 1971.

Hirschi, Travis. *Causes of Delinquency.* Berkeley: University of California Press, 1969.

Holt, John. *Escape from Childhood.* New York: Holt Associates, 1984.

Kramer, Rita. *At a Tender Age: Violent Youth and Juvenile Justice.* New York: Holt, Rinehart & Winston, 1988.

Le Shan, Eda. *The Roots of Crime.* New York: Four Winds Press, 1981.

Magid, Ken, and Carole A. McKelveyd. *High Risk: Children Without a Conscience.* New York: Bantam Books, 1988.

Mead, Margaret, and Martha Wolfenstein, eds. *Childhood in Contemporary Cultures.* Chicago: University of Chicago Press, 1963.

Moore, W. Joan, and Carlos Garcia. *Homeboys: Gangs, Drugs, and Prison in the Barrios of Los Angeles.* Philadelphia: Temple University Press, 1978.

National Conference of Charities and Correction. *History of Child Saving in the United States.* Montclair, NJ: Patterson Smith, 1971.

National Council of Jewish Women. *Children Without Justice.* New York: NCJW, N. d.

Nye, F. Ivan *Family Relationships and Delinquent Behavior.* Westport, CT: Greenwood Press, 1973.

Platt, Anthony M. *The Child Savers: The Invention of Delinquency.* Chicago: University of Chicago Press, 1980.

Quinney, Richard, ed. *Criminal Justice in America.* Boston: Little, Brown, 1974.

Rohr, Janelle, ed. *Violence in America: Opposing Viewpoints.* San Diego: Greenhaven Press, 1990.

Samenow, Stanton E. *Children and Crime: Why Some Kids Get in Trouble and What Parents Should Know About It.* New York: Times Books, 1989.

Sanders, Wiley B., ed. *Juvenile Offenders for a Thousand Years: Selected Readings from Anglo-Saxon Times to 1900.* Chapel Hill: University of North Carolina Press, 1969.

Schlossman, Steven L. *Love and the American Delinquent: The Theory and Practice of "Progressive" Juvenile Justice.* Chicago: University of Chicago Press, 1981.

Schwartz, Ira M. *(In)Justice for Juveniles: Rethinking the Best Interests of the Child.* Lexington, MA: Lexington Books, 1989.

Shaw, Clifford R. *Jack Roller: A Delinquent Boy's Own Story.* Chicago: University of Chicago Press, 1966.

Shoemaker, Donald J. *Theories of Delinquency: An Examination of the Explanation of Delinquent Behavior.* New York: Oxford University Press, 1984.

Sussman, Alan. *The Rights of Young People.* New York: Avon Books, 1981.

GLOSSARY

adjudication the process whereby a judge determines for which category of offense an individual should be tried

aggravated assault a violent attack on another person committed with criminal intent

assault a violent attack—or attempted attack—on another person

baby boomers the generation born during the 19 years (1946–64) following World War II, composing the largest age-group in the American population

blackjack a weapon consisting of a chain or piece of metal encased in leather

blasphemy a show of disrespect or ridicule for something that is considered sacred to others

cocaine the primary psychoactive ingredient obtained from the coca plant; a behavioral stimulant

crack a crystalline preparation of cocaine, usually smoked

delinquency offense conduct, such as burglary, committed by a juvenile, for which an adult would be prosecuted in a criminal court

demographers individuals who study and measure the statistical characteristics of human populations, such as its size, geographic distribution, and vital statistics

detention center a temporary residence for juveniles awaiting disposition in court

disposition the process in which a judge decides what must be done with an accused child—if the case should be dismissed, if the child should be referred to the care of a social agency, if he or she should be discharged and supervised by a court official, or if the child should be placed in a special institution for juvenile offenders

double jeopardy placing an individual on trial for a crime for which he or she has been previously tried

due process legal proceedings carried out in accordance with established rules and principles; in the United States, the accused must receive notice and charges, have a fair trial, be permitted to question those complaining against him or her, and be given an unbiased ruling based on the merits of the case

emancipation in juvenile law, release from the care and custody of one's parents or guardians

Fourteenth Amendment an addition to the Constitution that calls for due process of law and restrains state governments from restricting the privileges granted to all citizens of the United States

gang a group of youths who form a close-knit circle based on ties of allegiance; they often engage in violence to ensure their dominance over other gangs in a particular neighborhood

ghetto a section of a city populated almost exclusively by members of a specific minority group; social and economic pressures often create and perpetuate ghettos

hearing in juvenile justice, a court examination during which witnesses give their testimony

hedonism the belief that pleasure should be life's ultimate goal

homicide murder; the killing of one human being by another

illiteracy the inability to read or write

intake the first step in the juvenile court system in which the child's case is reviewed by a court official who decides whether or not the case should go through the official legal process or be dismissed

juvenile delinquency behavior by an individual under the age of 18 that is beyond parental control and therefore subject to legal action

machismo a strong, exaggerated sense of masculine pride

marijuana a psychoactive drug made from the crushed leaves, flowers, and branches of the hemp plant

parole the conditional release of a prisoner before completing his or her sentence

parens patriae a medieval English doctrine that permitted the British government to interfere in family matters when a child's welfare was at stake

pathological mentally or physically abnormal as a result of disease

penal relating to punishment

penitentiary a public institution used to detain violators of the law for an amount of time determined by a judge

probation the release of an individual from a penal institution under the supervision of a probation officer on the condition that he or she will maintain good behavior

probation officers individuals appointed by the courts to watch over offenders who have been released on probation

rehabilitation the act of restoring a criminal to normal social behavior

status offense conduct, such as running away from home, that is considered a crime only when it is performed by a juvenile

truancy staying out of school without permission

underclass the lowest social class

INDEX

PICTURE CREDITS

Ellen Heath Grinney is a 1967 graduate of Stanford University with a B.A. in English and has worked as a freelance writer in Houston, Texas, since 1987. She has had extensive experience researching and writing on national policy issues since 1973, when she began working on Capitol Hill in Washington, D.C. She served on the staffs of two congressmen and one senator, the Senate Banking Committee, and the Senate Republican Policy Committee. Upon moving to Houston in 1977, she developed a government relations program for an international manufacturing conglomerate. From 1984 through 1987, she was a manager of public affairs for the Methodist Hospital, the nation's largest private hospital.

Solomon H. Snyder, M.D., is Distinguished Service Professor of Neuroscience, Pharmacology, and Psychiatry and director of the Department of Neuroscience at the Johns Hopkins University School of Medicine. He has served as president of the Society for Neuroscience and in 1978 received the Albert Lasker Award in Medical Research for his discovery of opiate receptors in the brain. Dr. Snyder is a member of the National Academy of Sciences and a Fellow of the American Academy of Arts and Sciences. He is the author of *Drugs and the Brain*, *Uses of Marijuana*, *Madness and the Brain*, *The Troubled Mind*, and *Biological Aspects of Mental Disorder*. He is also the general editor of Chelsea House's ENCYCLOPEDIA OF PSYCHOACTIVE DRUGS.

C. Everett Koop, M.D., Sc.D., is former Surgeon General, deputy assistant secretary for health, and director of the Office of International Health of the U.S. Public Health Service. A pediatric surgeon with an international reputation, he was previously surgeon-in-chief of Children's Hospital of Philadelphia and professor of pediatric surgery and pediatrics at the University of Pennsylvania. Dr. Koop is the author of more than 175 articles and books on the practice of medicine. He has served as surgery editor of the *Journal of Clinical Pediatrics* and editor-in-chief of the *Journal of Pediatric Surgery*. Dr. Koop has received nine honorary degrees and numerous other awards, including the Denis Brown Gold Medal of the British Association of Paediatric Surgeons, the William E. Ladd Gold Medal of the American Academy of Pediatrics, and the Copernicus Medal of the Surgical Society of Poland. He is a chevalier of the French Legion of Honor and a member of the Royal College of Surgeons, London.